Control Room

A Barns-Miller

authorHOUSE®

AuthorHouse™ UK Ltd.
500 Avebury Boulevard
Central Milton Keynes, MK9 2BE
www.authorhouse.co.uk
Phone: 08001974150

First published by AuthorHouse 7/27/2009

ISBN: 978-1-4490-0504-7 (sc)

This book is printed on acid-free paper.

This book is dedicated to all Emergency Medical Dispatchers, certainly those I have worked alongside. We work very hard, we play all too little.

It is also dedicated to my family, especially my children, without whom there is no purpose. I love you, with all my heart.

Finally it is dedicated to Susan. Thank you for being my very best friend.

Acknowledgements

A special thank you to Tom's mum, Tina Campey. Thank you for your help with the publicising of this book.

Thank you to my friend and colleague, Angie who has been invaluable in her comments regarding the work

To my friends, the other regular 18 - 02's, Rachel, Louise and Jo in never complaining about being bored whilst listening about the book. Thank you for putting up with it!

Thanks also to all my family and friends who gave me the support and encouragement to accomplish a dream.

Finally, thanks to the Ambulance Service. Although the story contained in this book is totally fictitious, all ambulance staff across the world do an amazing and highly professional job of caring for patients and the community.   Thank you for allowing this book to be published.

Calling 999 for emergency medical help is, happily, something the vast majority of us will never do. However for those that do, help and advice is always available 24 hours a day, 7 days a week, 52 weeks a year.

Sadly, a percentage of these calls are not emergencies and control staff can be, and often are, verbally abused all too often.

More worryingly is the fact that ambulance front line personnel increasingly put themselves at risk from abuse and violence in their line of duty virtually every day.

However, should you need to, when dialling 999 for emergency medical help be prepared to give your telephone number and the address of the emergency along with the nature of the problem.

From the instant the address or location is taken, an emergency response is despatched immediately. You will not be delaying the help in any way by the questions you will be asked. These questions are of great importance regarding triaging the call. Advice will be given to assist the problem whilst help is on its way.

Whether a call is for a life or limb threatening situation, an imminent birth, or of a lesser emergency, you are the operator's eyes and they will guide you, if necessary giving life saving instructions and remain, where possible, with you, until a response is on scene.

The life of an ambulance Emergency Control Room is a busy one. It's the room that never sleeps. It's the hustle and bustle equivalent to Leicester Square or Kings Cross train stations. Where traffic becomes people and where voices are constantly heard. At the end of a twelve hour shift, there's satisfaction that many lives have been helped, saved and touched. Twelve hours together in one room is a very long time. Things change, circumstances change, people change. And for some of the Emergency Medical Call Operators and Dispatchers who work in this particular control centre, life might never be the same again......

Contents

Candice

DEEP IN HER HEART SHE nurtured a secret. She was playing a very dangerous game and she knew it. The danger of her secret being unveiled was something she knew could destroy lives but it was a game worth playing. It was a game she wanted to win and one she was determined not to lose.

Candice was a pretty girl. Striking looks with long waist length blond hair and legs that went on forever. Her cool blue eyes complimented her flawless complexion which needed no makeup. A natural beauty.

On the morning of her third shift of four she struggled to get out of bed. It was early and dark outside and she really didn't want to be getting up at all. As she swung her legs over the side of her warm and cosy bed she remembered the night before. She wrapped her naked arms around herself and fell back onto the pillows smiling, knowingly.

She closed her eyes to recall the time she had spent with him just hours before and of how wonderful it felt to be with him.

As she started to dream she was rudely awoken by the repeated shrill sound of the alarm clock telling her that this was her last chance to get up, get ready and get out. And she wondered how she ever got herself involved with him at all.

He was a lot older than her. Thirty two years older to be exact. And married with an eighteen year old daughter. But he was very, very good looking. He was also well off financially, although it was his wife that had all the money via an inheritance from her late father. His hair had turned a silver grey over the past two to three years but it made him appear distinguished, sophisticated and very suave. He was also tall, like her. He was generous, kind and he made her happy.

He had picked Candice up the previous evening, from her flat where she lived on the other side of the river. They had driven, chatting together about each other's day, to Candice's favourite restaurant where he had previously booked their usual table, in the alcove at the back, where it was quiet and dimly lit.

They were shown to their table and offered the menus, but Candice knew what she was going to have. She always did. Salmon to start, chicken wrapped in bacon on a bed of spinach and served with a cream and mushroom sauce with saute potatoes, French green beans and coffee to finish. Never desert. Desert meant calories. Calories meant weight on. The wine was bad enough for calories. It was one or the other - there was no contest, the wine won.

He preferred the meat option. His idea of food was food and to hell with the calories. So he ordered the steak, well done, and seasonable vegetables with extra chips, following the pate to start. And of course, a rather large choc-lately something or other to finish.

They discussed the weather, what they were missing on t.v. (she was heavily into Big Brother) and what the coming weekend could possibly have in store for them as they eat.

She adored being with him and he had great fun being with her, but fun was all it was, for him. After all he was married and was not prepared to put the past thirty years of hard graft obtaining the house he now no longer had a mortgage on in jeopardy. He wasn't going to risk losing that or his lavish lifestyle which was mainly funded by his wife. Plus, he might even loose his job and if he had no job, he would have no Mercedes Benz. In fact, he could lose it all. There was just too much at stake.

He was bought back down to earth by a chorus of laughter on the next table. The restaurant had filled up nicely since they had arrived and even though they were far enough away from home, he still felt uneasy once he became surrounded by people. People that might know him, worse still, might know his wife.

'Lets go' he smiled at Candice. 'I will pay the bill and then get you home, understand you are on an early shift in the morning?'

She looked dismayed. Disappointed that the evening was coming to an end. She looked so forward to being with him and being out with him was such a bonus. After all it had taken her a long time to convince him to venture out together, away from the safety of her flat, the flat purely funded by him. She loved being seen with him and although she knew it was dangerous for him, she knew he loved being seen with her, if nothing else, because of her beauty and radiance. As long as they weren't being seen by anyone he might know.

He paid the bill and escorted her out of the restaurant to the car for the lengthy journey back home to her flat. His car was top of the range and cost the price of a small mortgage. She loved being in it. It made her feel rich, as he was. She would often wish she was Mrs Mike Jenkins and would often daydream about being so. It was never going to happen of course. He would never leave her.

The wife was the same age as him but the years had not been so gracious to her. She was quite short, plump and had a very aged and wrinkled neck. She was different in every way to Candice and she often wondered if that was what attracted him to her, being so very different. Old crab, as she was secretly called by Candice, was at the opposite end of the scale. Old crab didn't work. No, she didn't have to get up at five in the morning to be at work for seven, to endure a twelve hour day long shift. Old crab would instead sleep in to about ten or eleven and after breakfast at that rather exclusive health club with some other crustaceans would spend hours being pampered from head to toe only to emerge not looking any different at all.

Candice had only seen her once. And that was by mistake.

She had gone into London for some Christmas shopping at the end of the previous year. It was while she was perusing the perfumery counter wondering which perfume her mother would prefer when she saw him from the corner of her eye.

Excitedly she had gone to say hello when she realised that with him was his wife. She felt total resentment and jealously as she had never experienced previously. He looked, as if he had been taken off guard, nervous in fact. He held his breath wondering if Candice would do anything stupid. What was she doing here, this is where they shopped, not her. This was 'their' store. And for a moment he felt resentment and jealously, but for different reasons.

Candice stopped in her tracks, but couldn't help stare at the woman whom she had always envisaged to be glamorous, beautiful and upright. Instead what she saw in front of her was a woman totally the opposite. Candice was shocked, if not astounded. And then she felt anger. She was angry that this woman was not more like her. She knew then that there was no competition, but she wanted there to be. She wanted to feel at least he had embarked upon an affair with an equal to his spouse rather than a total opposite. Was this why he wanted to be with her, that she was so different to the old crab?

She let them walk past her and she carried on pondering the perfumes. Dior won. Once they had passed her by she purchased her gift, turned on her heel and left. She headed in the direction of the nearest boutique for some retail therapy trying hard not to let tears of jealousy appear.

He had been angry with her that she had been in the wrong place at the wrong time. He had telephoned her on his mobile immediately upon his return to his home, when the wife was busy engaged in some pointless telephone conversation with one of her yoga friends.

'What the hell were you doing in London earlier. I thought you were going to say something. You know if you had then that would have been it, don't you?' His voice was hard, not at all the voice she was used to.

'I, I'm sorry' came her weak reply, taken off guard. There was silence was a few seconds and then he just simply said 'I'll call you'.

'Candice?' The voice bought her back.

'Sorry, Mike, what was that?'
'I said are you o.k - you seem a little distant?'

'Yeah, I'm fine, just a little tired'. She paused. 'You coming in for a little while?' she asked as they pulled in the car park that was at the back of the flats where she lived.

'You stop me' he smiled. 'You just stop me!' And he squeezed her knee fondly.

They left the car and quietly approached the main door of Cambrose Court, where, for the next hour at least she would have him all to herself and pretend that he was hers entirely.

—

The shrill ring of the alarm clock rang once more and startled her out of her semi slumber. She knew that if she remained in bed for a moment longer she would be late for work so she quickly showered and dressed and applied a lick of mascara before grabbing her keys, slamming shut the door, 'sorry neighbours' she whispered, as it was still very early, and left for her car.

The drive to work took approximately twenty minutes. She hummed along to the tunes of Kiss on the radio and at times sang out loud to her favourite tunes.

After parking her Clio in the staff car park she briskly waltzed up to the canteen where she bought a coffee and wandered back down to the control centre where she would be for the next twelve hours at least.

'Hi guys' she said cheerily as she pushed open the heavily door which lead her to the foyer where the morning's shift staff were waiting.

'Last one again, Candice' laughed Polly.

Polly was another call operator in the centre. She was a very sweet girl, only eighteen and had recently joined them after completing her six week long training course.

Candice rolled her eyes upward and laughed back. 'Where are you going to sit?' she enquired of her new friend. 'By the window?' Polly replied. 'OK, lets go then'. And the morning's shift handed over from the previous night.

Candice settled herself down next to Polly and logged onto the computer. She plugged her earphones in to the telephone connection and placed her head set in position, waving happily at other operators who were either leaving after their shift or those like her who were about to start.

'Ambulance, Emergency, what's the address of the emergency?' came a voice in the distance as another operator started to take her first emergency call of the day.

'Ambulance Service' she heard Polly say and Polly started to talk to the first of many doctors or doctors' receptionists she was certainly going be speaking to that day.

The doctor was telephoning to admit an elderly gentleman who had during the night fallen unwell due to some form of urinary tract infection and was now appearing to become confused, possibly due to a high temperature that the UTI would have caused.

Candice heard him behind her.

'Morning everyone' said the familiar voice of the call centre manager.

'Morning Candice' he purposely added. She turned her head around.

She smiled. She twirled round in her chair to fully face him and watch him walk slowly to his office. 'Morning Mike' she answered. And then she got her first call.

Polly

ONE OF THE LATEST IN a batch of new recruits to the Centre. There were six in all that made it through the interview process and the same six started on the same day.

She had it on good authority that she would 'walk' the interview and that the entrance examination would be easy for her as she was bright, very clever and had only just left school after remaining on in the sixth form. After all, he should know. He was always right.

The interview was, as promised, fine but she did struggle with the exam. There were several parts to it and she seemed to have been in the building where it took place all day, although it had only been four hours.

Obviously when you have the lives of people in your hands you have to be of some form of calibre, have some level of intelligence but you also have to have something else, something that they are looking for. That something is to have an understanding, to be calm and remain so in every situation, to be able to empathise rather than sympathise and compassion. Compassion is very important.

Therefore the way you conduct yourself in that interview is of vast importance. To be able to demonstrate what they require. And to be able to complete the exam. In the multiple choice paper they tell you that no answer is the right one. What they mean is that they will analyse those answers and conclude from them what kind of person you are. Then they will know if you are what they want, what they need and if you would be suitable.

The written maths test was the one she had difficulty with but she was allowed a calculator and, because she finished in time, was able to go back through her answers, correcting them when she felt she should. She handed it in feeling very unsure about her mark.

The man in the green ambulance uniform collected the papers thanking each and every person in the room. Out of the twenty three sitting only six would pass to go through.

They were told to go out through the larger of the two doors to the left of the room and make their way to the restaurant where they could help themselves to fresh coffee and biscuits which had been laid out for them specially.

Polly grabbed her handbag by her feet and made her way out with the others. Once in the restaurant they all sighed in relief that it was over and all congratulated each other as to that fact.

Polly got talking to a young boy called Griff. His name was Gordon Griffiths but he hated his first name so made everyone address him by his nickname.

Griff was eighteen, just like Polly. He had remained in the sixth form at school before contemplating on a possible career within the ambulance service. He did think about university to study as a paramedic but decided that if he passed the interview then that was what fate intended for him and he would in time progress via the control room.

They got on very well, although Polly thought he was a little too sure of himself, a little too cocky for her liking.

On her first day of the training she sat with Griff, both unbelieving of the fact that they had both got through and so many hadn't. The others in the course were also amazed that they too had manage to pass. One girl said she was sure she had blown it as she had found out that when asked what was an 'acute abdomen' she had written her reply as 'nice flat stomach'.

The people marking the papers must have had a good sense of humour.

The training course was tough but very enjoyable. It lasted six weeks and in that time they learnt about the ambulance service, about who did what, and were introduced to many directors and management they would probably never meet again.

They also spent three weeks in an exhausting medical training schedule. They were taught about the patient care chain of survival, the heart and respiratory system, about the body as a whole, including the skeleton, about CPR (cardio pulmonary resuscitation), defibrillation, about strokes, to continue with the general functions of the emergency medical dispatcher (EMD).

The following week was used to demonstrate real life scenarios, for role play and for tests. Tests to show that what had been explained had been absorbed.

Finally the remaining week was used to explain the computerised medical system which is used by the majority of ambulance services throughout Britain, Europe, Canada, Australia and the USA, where it was introduced.

More tests were undertaken by the young hopefuls and only upon successful completion of these were they allowed to practice what they had learnt. They were now qualified EMDs and now each and every one of them held the certification that legally enabled them to work in the control centre and any control centre in the world that practiced it.

They all went out to celebrate at the local Tapas restaurant. Excited about their future careers, congratulated on their achievement, for it isn't easy getting through and only the best do.

On her first day from training Polly was assigned to Candice. They, who make the decisions as to who is paired with who, do so for the reasons of experience of the 'buddy' or 'mentor' and personality. It was believed they would be perfect together.

And so they were.

She had completed the expected two weeks mentoring with Candice and did so wonderfully.

Although there were eight years between them it was as if there was no age gap at all as the two girls got on so well.

It was Polly's last day of mentoring and Candice had suggested they go out for a drink after work for she wasn't sure when they would next work together as shifts change.

At 19.00, after the girls had handed over to the night shift they left the building.

They started off in the little wine bar just down the road. It was quiet when they arrived and they had a bottle of wine between them whilst chatting excitedly about the past couple of weeks together.

The bar started to fill up so they decided to move on down to the end of the high street as there was a small Italian restaurant hidden away between the florists and the Co-Op. It was cheap and the food was very good.

They ordered another bottle of wine but as Candice was driving she didn't touch a drop of it. In fact she was a little worried about the amount of alcohol Polly was consuming and so quickly.

However they ordered their food and continued their conversation.

'Have you got a man then Candice?' Polly enquired. 'Well, er, yes. Suppose I have'. 'Suppose?' mocked Polly, who was becoming a little loud at this stage.

'Yes', Candice quickly added. 'I don't see him much, he, er, works away you see'. 'Oh', came Polly's response. Candice knew the truth must never come out.

'I don't have one, yet' Polly added. 'Hope that I might pick one of those paramedics up!' Candice smiled.

The food came and they started to eat. Candice watched her young friend. She thought for a moment, just one moment that she reminded her ever so slightly of someone. The eyes, that look. She was just about to ask a question when Polly at that point knocked over a glass of wine. It fell to the floor and smashed into what seemed like a million pieces.

'Oops, I'm sorry', I didn't, see it there' and then she broke out in a fit of giggles which Candice found highly contagious.

They both laughed out loud although, Candice found herself apologising profusely to the small dark haired harassed waiter that seemed to have been assigned to clear up the mess.

'I think, we ought to pay and better go' Candice smiled at Polly who by this stage was screwing up her face and closing one eye so that she could focus better.

'Come on, I'll take you home. You better not live too far though' she said to Polly, helping her out of the restaurant. Candice knew Polly couldn't have lived too far away. She used the train to get her to and from work. Even though its favourable to drive, its not essential. And Polly was hoping to start driving lessons once she was earning some money. She had often remarked that she had asked her parents who apparently were 'loaded' to help her pay for them but they had flatly refused. 'Tight gits' thought Candice.

They managed to get back to the car, Candice trying her best to keep Polly from swaying around too much. 'You drank too much far too quickly', she said to Polly in a rather motherly fashion. 'You'll have one hell of a headache tomorrow'.

'Right then' said Candice as she helped Polly with the seat belt. 'Which way?'

Polly struggled with her words but eventually managed to spit out a garbled address totally incomprehensible to Candice.

'Oh dear' thought Candice. 'This could end up being a long night'.

'Polly, if you don't tell me your address, I shall leave you here' threatened Candice. Although she would never have in a million years done such a thing, she thought it might be the only way to get some sense out of her drunken counterpart.

'Sands Hill Drive' came the instant response. 'That did the trick then', thought Candice as she pondered on the address just given as that it was one of the most expensive roads in the County. 'Erm, are you sure you live in Sands Hill Drive?' Candice enquired.

'Yep, 15 Sands Hill, hic, Drive'. 'O.K, then' replied a bemused Candice. 'This should be interesting' she whispered to herself. And she started the engine.

They drove out of the space they had found earlier and started their drive along the High Street, past the wine bar and the restaurant where they had both spent the time since leaving the Centre. She turned right at the mini roundabout and continued forward towards to the main road which lead them out of the town and towards the rather exclusive part of the County which Polly had instructed she drive to.

Twenty minutes later they pulled into the tree lined road. The houses were large, detached and very expensive. There were BMWs, Jaguars, 4 x 4s and Porsches parked in driveways. She drove slowly, not just so that she could make out which one of these absolutely gorgeous properties belonged to her drunken and now fast asleep friend but to admire the absolute beauty and vastness of these houses.

No. 15 was set back from the road. It was double fronted and must have had at least seven if not eight bedrooms. 'I hope you have got this correct.' muttered Candice as she pulled up outside. 'You better not be having a laugh' she continued through gritted teeth. Polly had fallen asleep during the journey, so Candice woke her, albeit abruptly.

She got out of the car and opened the passenger side door so that Polly could fall straight out onto the pavement. 'Ouch' came Polly's instant awakened response. 'Oops, sorry' Candice giggled, 'You alright?   Need an ambulance?' she playfully asked.

'Nope, I - shall - be - fine. Don't - know - what - my - parents will say though' came the slow, carefully spoken response from Polly, who was now feeling extremely sick.

Candice supported her drunken pal up the seemingly non ending drive. There was obviously someone, thankfully, at home as some of the windows were open.

'Amazing' Candice said to herself. 'Absolutely bloody amazing'. She had never seen a house like it. It was huge, and beautiful. Candice rang the bell to No 15 Sands Hill Drive.

She waited a while, which seemed an age, and then pressed the bell again before she heard the footsteps approach. Candice felt a bit guilty and embarrassed by this stage. Here she was, supporting this girl to remain in the upright position whom it must appear she had got totally intoxicated, handing her over to her obviously rich family. It wasn't done deliberately, it wasn't .... the door opened. She quickly stared at Polly, took a huge breath and turned her head to meet the eyes of the unsuspecting parent.

And with absolute shock and horror spat ...... 'Mike!'

Belinda

THE SUPERVISOR'S JOB WAS TO oversee everything that happens either in the dispatch part or the call operator part of the control room. There are countless reports and decisions to be made. Usually to become a supervisor vast experience is gained in both call operating and dispatch and after proving you have the necessary experience and skills you would then perhaps be considered for the role although further exams and a presentation had to be passed.

Belinda had been with the service for eighteen years, working both in the call centre and then in dispatch, allocating and sending vehicles to emergencies before her promotion.

She was in her early forties and very well liked. She had a short bob which flicked out at the ends and her eyes were brown to match her hair. She had a pretty face and was extremely thin but then that's how she liked to be.

She had been married for twelve years to Rob, a paramedic. The marriage had broken down some eighteen months previously and they had separated. Having no children the divorce was simple and easy but living on her own was something she did not find easy. And she missed him.

After the divorce she absorbed herself in as much overtime as possible and read a lot. She found living alone difficult, lonely, and at times she regretted the fact that they never had a baby for she believed that at her age she would never now be in a position to bare a child. She tried hard to not think on what might have been for she found it depressing, let alone pointless, but there were times when she would absorb herself with meaningless regret.

After her marriage to Rob she had been diagnosed with breast cancer and for the coming weeks and months he had helped her overcome her fears and had help her back to full strength. She had been lucky. They had found the tumour in time and had removed it. She had been in remission and had come out the other side with a clean bill of health.

They were so happy then. Why did he have to go and spoil it all by having that fling with that girl? Why did he have to go and spoil it all? Was she not enough for him? Not pretty enough or thin enough? Or was it that her illness had got too much for him? These were all questions she fired over and over again at him but got very little response apart from he was sorry and he didn't know why.

After his affair they did try to carry on as normal, as if it had never occurred, but Belinda just couldn't accept it had happened. She kept picturing the two of them together and each time she did it would make her cry and lash out at him again and again.

He didn't exactly break the news very well to her. It was New Years Eve and they were to go to a party. She was delighted that for the first time in three years she had got New Years eve off from work, therefore she was going to enjoy every minute. He had gone out previously promising he would be back in plenty of time. She had been in the bath for hours and put on her make up and that very expensive little black number that she had only just bought. She couldn't understand what was keeping him. She had rung him on his mobile several times but it was off.

It was now gone nine and they should have left by now. Where was he, was he alright, what if he had been involved in an accident? All these questions were probing her thoughts and her mind was playing tricks with her. She was just thinking of telephoning control to see if any car accidents had occurred within the past couple of hours when she heard his key in the door.

'Where have you been?' she cried anxiously, jumping up from the sofa and approaching him with her arms outstretched. 'Bel, come and sit down' he said. He looked drawn, tired, 'there's something I need to tell you'. 'Oh, God' she replied, 'I don't like the sound of this!'.

He took both her hands and sat her on the cream leather settee. Sitting next to her and still holding her hands gently he told her of how sometimes, things happen. You don't go out looking for them, they just do.

She looked at him quietly, with a puzzled expression. He continued.

'Some time ago, I did something I shouldn't have' he went on to say, his eyes now looking downward. He took a long and thoughtful breath. 'I've been having an affair with a girl I met some time ago. I have tried to end it several times but tonight I did. That's where I have been. I ended it because I want to be with you. However, she told me that if I did, if I ended it, then she would tell you. I didn't want you to hear it from her, I would rather you heard it from me'.

'You, you had an affair?' Belinda softly whispered. 'Yes' he gently replied.

Her brown eyes silently pleading with him. 'No, please don't do this' she quietly begged.

'I'm so sorry, Bel, if I could have stopped it I would have'.

'Stopped it, STOPPED IT?' she screamed at him. 'Why even START it in the first place?' She pulled her hands away from him and slapped him hard with the full brunt of the palm of her hand and then she started to cry. Tears of absolute disbelief started to trickle down her pale face. She put her head in her hands and sobbed. She cried like she had never cried before. Her perfect world in which she had the perfect life, the perfect house and the perfect marriage. It was as if everything she held dear was being crushed.

He stood up and looked down at her. 'I'm sorry' he softly said. And then he quietly left.

It was March. The buds on some of the trees were beginning to appear and because there had been some unusually warm days, some flowers were popping up too.

She wandered around her small flat, tidying. She was off that day, a rest day, so she had plenty of time to clean. And clean is really all she ever did now. It seemed a very long time since that dark New Year's eve. And she missed him. She STILL missed him.

She recalled his confession that New Year's eve after which he had stayed away for a few days. She wondered constantly where he was and, more importantly, who he was with. Was he with her? What was she like? Where did she live? Did she know her? How long had it been going on? All the questions seemed to have no answers.

She had stayed at home since his confession and had called in sick under compassionate grounds to the control centre. She would tell them all eventually, but not today. After all they were, as a couple, so well known to everyone there. There was no way she could manage to go into work and face everybody. They would all know as the pain was etched across her face, a face so full of sadness and sorrow. She wasn't fit for duty and she wasn't even able to get dressed.

She had sat, day and night, thinking, not sleeping, smoking cigarette after cigarette watching the smoke curl round and round making patterns in her deep thought and sadness, a sadness she had never known she would ever feel. She hated feeling like it.

She remembered back to the night of his confession and how she hadn't eaten properly. She hadn't changed from her blue dressing gown that she had been wearing since taking off that dress. The dress that had cost a fortune. That dress that she would never, ever want to wear again. She hadn't even cleaned her teeth. She looked in the mirror that was above the mantle-piece above the fire. It was a beautiful mirror that was adorned by an ornate brass surround. They had chosen it together, a year ago. They had gone to the January sales and seen it in a window of a large and fashionable department store. They hadn't intended buying a mirror but they both loved it and knew they just had to have it. Again her tears fell silently, slowly down her cheeks. She brushed them away with her left hand. A hand that still had a gold band on its fourth finger.

She looked drawn. Tired. Older. She looked away, not wanting to see her reflection, the reflection of a woman betrayed, of a woman broken.

Eventually she reached for her mobile phone. She hesitated, just for a moment, but then she dialled it and heard the ring at the other end.

'Belinda?' The response was just one word, her name, but it was full of question, concern and anticipation.

'Yes' she firmly replied. 'I need to speak to you. Can you come home around seven this evening?' 'Oh, and don't think you are staying. I just want some answers'.

She pressed the disconnect button on the phone and threw it gently down onto the chair beside her.

She looked at the clock. The clock that had been watching her, minute after minute, ticking its annoying tick, tick, tick. It was 3. She decided to take a bath and get dressed.

At a minute to the hour he was expected she heard his key turn in the door. He approached, looking as drawn and as tired as she felt.

He didn't get to even sit down before her first question was fired at him.

'Who is it? I need to know her name and also exactly how long has this been going on, behind my back?'

'Not long, six months. Look it doesn't mater who it is Bel, its over. She meant nothing'

'SIX MONTHS? How could you? So you're not going to tell me then? Am I not worth the truth? Lets face it had she not threatened to tell me then it might not be over, I might not even know, surely you have the decency to tell me who she is, I deserve that much'

'Theres no point Bel, I am not going to tell you. Look, it was a mistake. Its over now, can't we just go back to how we were?'

'I don't think so. I need some time. Its best if you leave. You obviously want to protect her. I am not so sure if I like that'. He had left after gathering some belongings and she tried very hard to conceal the fact that her heart was breaking. But he knew her and he knew the damage that he had caused. He knew he had broken her.

They had, after a couple more weeks, got together again. He had written to her, in his spell binding and romantic way that first drew her to him. He had told her how sorry he was, that he had made a mistake and that he loved her, more than anything in the world. He begged forgiveness and asked if they could give it one more try. He asked if they could pretend it never happened, blot it out. He said he would make it up to her in what ever way she wanted.

She succumbed and he moved back in. It didn't last long. She couldn't accept his betrayal, she tried but as much as she adored him, loved him entirely, it just wasnt working. They decided to separate and eventually divorce. It was a sad day for them both and it was a sad day for everyone that knew them as a couple.

She was used to the calls in the centre, the constant overdoses and self harmers, even the jumpers and the odd hangings. She had often wondered what drove people to harm themselves or consider taking their own lives. And now, today, she was considering that too.

She walked to the kitchen cupboard where her medicines were kept and took the large bottle of unopened paracetamol. Next to it was some sleeping tablets the doctor had prescribed all that time ago when Rob had left her and which she had never taken, but kept. She had taken one or two then but the rest remained. She counted them out. Forty eight were clasped within her palm. She carried them through to the lounge with the paracetamol. She sat down, opened another bottle of wine and poured herself another glass.

She had never drank alcohol before lunchtime, let alone 8 am. But this was different. This would be her last glass. She emptied the paracetamol into her palm. There were 96 in all but she could only swallow a few at a time. When they were all gone she started on the sleeping tablets until they too had been swallowed along with the wine.

'No more pain' she whispered to herself.

She then took Rob's picture with her and laid on the bed holding him close to her. 'Night, babe' she whispered. 'I love you'. And before long she was asleep.

The telephone had been ringing but there was no answer. Her mobile phone had been switched off and she hadn't appeared for duty at work. After another couple of shifts of her non appearance people were beginning to get suspicious that something was wrong.

Mike had taken the decision to drive round, just to check if everything was alright.

Rob has also been trying her. Even though they were apart they still had contact and he knew they still loved each other, but the damage, his damage, had been done. He had been into the office earlier that day and spoken to Mike, enquiring where she was, this woman who was always at work, always reliable.

Her car was outside and the curtains in the flat were drawn, even though it was day time. Mike had tried the doorbell but no answer. He then decided to call the police.

Two burly police officers arrived and after a short conversation with Mike agreed to break in and enter the flat.

They found her, as she had laid, on the bed clasping the photograph that meant so much to her, the man that meant everything to her and that she would never have again. The man that would now have to live the rest of his life full of remorse and regret.

An ambulance was called. She was pronounced dead at the scene having choked on her own vomit following the overdose.

The Funeral

WORD OF HER DEATH QUICKLY spread around the control room. Everyone there was in a state of disbelief and shock.

Mike had returned to the Centre ashen faced. As he walked through the corridor to his office he was aware of a voice asking him if all was well with Belinda, did he speak to her, was she alright? He didn't answer but kept walking - into his office and closed the door and telephoned first Rob and then Personnel.

The email went out within the hour. It read:

Dear All,

I have the dreadful task of having to inform you all that at 1pm today Belinda Sweetman was pronounced dead at her flat. I do not know the details of her untimely death but it appears she may have taken her own life. The police have informed me that they will be conducting informal interviews with us all in an attempt to try and find out what might have happened and why she might have taken this sort of drastic action.

Rob Sweetman has been contacted as she has no other living relatives and I have asked that he advise me as soon as possible regarding the funeral arrangements so I can release as many of you as possible that may wish to attend.

I know that many of you were very fond of Belinda and she was well respected within the Service. She will be dreadfully missed.

Mike.

A couple of the girls were in tears, unable to take in the news. A sudden quiet fell upon the room and as if by some form of coincidence, for once the phones were silent.

Mike emerged from his office glancing at Candice who was wiping a tear from her face. He too had been crying.

The day came. Cover from another call centre within the neighbouring county was bought in and 100% of those asking for leave were given authority to attend the funeral.

The confirmed information that Belinda's death was caused by an overdose was very hard for Rob to accept. He was enormously wrapped up in remorse and guilt. His eyes were red from the crying he had been doing and he wasn't alone.

The black limousine made it's slow journey towards the large group awaiting its arrival. A man wearing black attire with a top hat was walking in front. Slowly, slowly it approached and as it did, the group retreated to the chapel for the service.

The oak coffin was carried in by members of the undertaker company. It was laid before them, an enormous and beautiful oasis of white lilies and roses adorned it. Rob had requested that the florist give instructions to the undertaker that it was to be placed upon the casket, after all, it would be the very last time he ever bought her anything. For the girl that adored arum lilies and white roses together, it made sense he should buy them for her. The final present.

Soft classical music was being played in the background amongst muffled sobs. He was to speak, soon, and then her song would be played. The song she loved and he had bought it for her, because she had loved it.

The Minister had given a reading although Rob didn't hear any of it. All he could think of as he sat there in the front row staring constantly at her final resting bed was of how badly he had treated her. He had loved her. He had just made a mistake, that's all. And it cost them both in the end.

The Minister was indicating to Rob that he should approach the front. He slowly stood and walked towards where the Minister was moving away from, so that he could say the few words he needed to be heard. A sea of people in green ambulance uniforms ahead of him were friends and acquaintances known to them both .

He quietly started to speak, engulfed by his sadness and sorrow.

'We shouldn't be here, you and I. And I feel I have a big part to play in Belinda's decision to take her own life. However, I have to live with that for the rest of MY life. As for Belinda, she was such a beautiful lady. A kind and genuine person. I am honoured to have been part of her time in this world.

She was a strong and courageous lady. She overcame cancer many years ago as some of you already know. She fought the disease with a determination that puts me to shame, a strong courage I wish I had right now.

If I could go back in time I would change things. But its too late. There's no point in regret. Regret is a useless and empty word. But I have to use the word regret. There is no other. I regret our splitting up. I regret hurting her the way I did when I told her that I had been unfaithful. The look in her eyes is a look that will haunt me forever. And that will be my punishment until the day I die.

She is at rest now, away from any more turmoil and pain. I hurt her, I know that and I will hate myself forever. I am so, so sorry Bel.

I have never, ever loved anyone as much as I loved Belinda. In fact I have never loved anyone else. If I could have her back for just one moment to tell her that again, I would give anything.

Sleep well, Belinda. Until I see you again, I love you. I will always love you. You will be in my heart forever'.

———

The Minister, and a couple of their colleagues stepped forward to comfort the shaking and distressed ex-husband and helped him back to his seat.

The music had started. The song by Lionel Richie was softly being played. It was the song they danced to at their wedding reception. The curtain surrounding her coffin was closing. Then she was gone.

His note he had instructed to be placed with the flowers that laid on the casket simply read,

'Forgive me. I will love you forever. Until I see you again, sleep well babe, Rob xxx'

'*Three Times A Lady*'

'Thanks for the times that you've given me,
The memories are all in my mind.
And now that we've come to the end of our rainbow
There's something I must say out loud.

You're once, twice, three times a lady, and I love you,
Yes you're once, twice, three times a lady,
And I love you, I love you.

When we are together the moments I cherish,
With every beat of my heart.
To touch you, to
hold you, to feel you, to need you.
There's nothing to keep us apart.

Yes, you're once, twice, three times a lady,
And I love you, I love you'.

(L. Richie)

Griff

FAIR AND PLAIN LOOKING, COCKY, but with an extremely good sense of humour, Griff got on very well with everyone he worked with. He was constantly clowning about and playing practical jokes and he turned out to be someone you certainly needed to have near you should you be experiencing a particularly bad day.

He had trained with Polly and had been mentored by Bernice, another call operator, who although was exceedingly good at her job and well experienced, was crap at having a laugh.

He had no intention of remaining within the Centre. He wanted out on the road. He was told he would have to remain within the control centre at least six months before he could even think of completing an application form for a trainee paramedic's post. He would have to pass his probationary period for one thing and prove himself within the role he had been trained for.

His mentoring was now over and he was taking calls by himself, although like all other new recruits he was surrounded by senior EMDs just in case he experienced any difficulties.

The bleep came into his right ear.

'Ambulance Emergency', he said. 'What's the address of the emergency?'

The hysterical woman was screaming loudly that she needed an ambulance. Griff used his firm but calm techniques which had been expertly taught in getting her to give the address of the emergency he so desperately needed so that a response could be dispatched.

It transpired that her six month old baby had stopped breathing. The worst case scenario to many call operators. It was his first resuscitation call.

Calmly and professionally he asked the questions he needed to gain the all important information as to how best he could deal with the situation and give medical instructions, knowing he must keep her with him until the crew arrived on scene.

The mother of the child was extremely and understandably frightened, panicked and inconsolable but he kept with her, repeating each stage of the resuscitation instructions softly but firmly.

Once or twice she became hysterical again and he needed to use his knowledge of being in control of the call to get her to listen to him, to understand him and to act on what he was instructing.

Seconds before the crew arrived on scene, he heard the baby gasp for air and cry.

He didn't know if he wanted to laugh or cry. It was the best sound he had ever heard, along with the sirens that had approached her home, and the baby's mother, through her sobs of relief, couldn't stop thanking him, over and over again.

Unbeknown to him, during the whole of the call, he had been shadowed by Bernice who had, because of her many years of experience, noticed immediately what Griff was up against. Being his first life and death situation for real she quickly arose from her chair and stayed behind him for the duration of the call just in case he got into difficulty. She shouldn't have worried for he handled the call perfectly and just as is should have been, the brilliant training kicking into effect. She quietly returned to her chair without Griff even realising she had been there, in the background observing.

The first resuscitation call is always the worst, a baby or child is even more so.

—

During lunch he had struck up a conversation with Polly when Bernice walked over to their table, much to his annoyance as he was enjoying having Polly to himself. Bernice sat down with that miserable face of hers that, in his words, looked like a 'slapped arse'.

'Erm, hi Bernice' said Polly. 'You alright?'

'Yeah, I'm alright. Well done with that call earlier, by the way' she directed towards Griff.

He nodded in polite thanks.

'Been trying to get in and see Mike all day, about that management course I want to get on, but he's been busy all the time' she continued.

Polly smiled at her in silent understanding. She knew only too well that once her father was engrossed in something you didn't get a look in. He didn't like interruptions, he was like that at home too, but she couldn't let them know that of course, she couldn't let on the truth that he was her father as it would probably go against her. People would think that she was given the job rather than got it on her own merits and also she would lose respect amongst those that she had come to like and get on well with and people would stop trusting her for fear that she would be repeating what she might have overheard.

Griff excused himself from the table as he obviously wasn't going to be allowed to spend any more time with Polly.

'She'll wait for another day' he silently thought.

While he took the walk back to the Control Room he was thinking to himself that he was going to be the one that got on the course, not Bernice. And if he had to fight for a place, then he would fight and use whatever tactics he could.

The Mechanic And Stephanie

HE WALKED INTO THE CONTROL Room with a kind of cocky swagger. He had been an 'in-house' mechanic for just a few weeks but had settled into his role well, liked by his colleagues and very good at his job.

Stephanie was a dispatcher. She very rarely took emergency calls from the public, her job was to dispatch the response once a call was logged onto the system.

She kept to herself much of the time, although she was popular. Married with three children she had a busy life - working twelve hour shifts, seeing to the children, two boys and a girl and arranging childcare when it was not possible for her to attend to them. On top of that she had a house to care for and a very miserable marriage.

Her husband was nine years her senior. He rarely worked and she spent a lot of her time clearing up after him, and making excuses for him. Their marriage was an empty and a pointless one but she stayed in it for the sake of the children. She had decided that once the children had grown up and left home she would leave him, before many more years slipped away and she would be faced with an uncertain and miserable future.

It had not always been this way. When they met he was a was working for a successful printing firm within the printing industry. Eventually he broke away and started his own company. They were happy and comfortable.

The business had been very successful and before having the children they had bought a beautiful home, furnishing it with antique furniture and had been on several exotic holidays together and then as a family .

However a recession had hit and the business had started to lose money. He had managed to keep a few of his staff but many of them had been made redundant.

Within six months the liquidators had been called in. He no longer worked, he didn't want to and spent most of his days moping around the house, knocking back the whisky at times. They had managed to keep their home and everything within it but now she was the breadwinner, she was the wife, the mother, the nurse, the gardener, the cook, the cleaner, the taxi driver. And she was resentful.

She carried on, for the children. At least they weren't babies any longer.

She passed him on her way to the rest room. She caught his glance and smiled at him. The smile was returned and she felt him turn and watch her as she walked on.

Later that day as she was about to get into her car for the drive back home she noticed that she had a flat tyre. She approached the workshop which was just about to close down and noticed that he was there. Her heart skipped a couple of beats as she approached him from behind. How sexy he was in those overalls, the arms of the outfit now wrapped around his middle and he was now bare chested   His bare flesh bronzed and toned. Her daydream was quickly quashed when he turned to her.

'Hello you' he happily said. 'What brings you in here?'

'I, erm, my flat has a tyre' she spat out in total panic thinking that he might be able to read her thoughts.

'Think you mean that to be that your tyre has a flat?' he teased her.

They laughed together and walked towards her vehicle. 'No problem, I'll fix it for you. Got the keys?' She handed over her keys and stood silently back while he expertly repaired the puncture.

It didn't take very long. He worked quickly and had the car driveable within minutes. She found herself wishing that her engine had blown up and she would be stuck there with him for hours, if not days …. If not weeks.

'Thank you so much' she said as he handed back the keys. 'I don't know what I would have done if you hadn't been here' she said and nervously smiled.

'No worries, call me if ever you need me' he jokingly replied, smiling. She turned and walked towards the vehicle feeling him watching her every step behind her, wanting to turn and smile again at him, wanting to go back and impulsively throw her arms around his neck and kiss him, slowly, passionately, she knew that these were ridiculous thoughts. After all he must be at least ten years her junior, and she was married for goodness sake. She dismissed the thoughts she was experiencing. And then she was in her car and on her way.

However, all the journey home she kept hearing his voice in her head, 'call me if ever you need me'. Did he really mean it, could it be that he was interested in her, or was that just the kind of man he was?

She knew she wanted to find out. And she knew at that point she would do everything in her power to.

—

She spent the coming days dreaming about the gorgeous mechanic. She found herself feeling like she did many years ago as a teenager and daydreaming about him. She knew she couldn't be distracted during her work and she tried very hard to put him to the back of her mind whilst carrying out her role but it was extremely difficult and hard to do.

But for once in a very long time she felt whole, she felt happy inside.

Her life was such a shambles at home, living in a loveless relationship, she felt revitalised and had some purpose now. She knew she would have to make the first move if she wanted to take things onto another level but she was frightened. She was scared that she would make a fool of herself, scared that the mechanic probably behaved in that way to every female he encountered and scared that her work colleagues might find out and cause her a problem.

After all, this wasn't the first time she had embarked upon an affair. It got nasty in the end and she ended up losing him, but it could have been so much worse. She could have lost a lot more. Besides, it had taught her a lesson, in having an affair and getting away with it, didn't it?

However, she dismissed the doubts and niggling worries. After all she was entitled to a life, some fun - wasn't she? She had sacrificed so much these past years and had worked hard to get and keep their home and their possessions.

She knew there would probably be no future in anything that may happen with the mechanic but then she had no future at home either, what had she got to lose? 'Absolutely nothing' she said out loud.

'Excuse me?' came a voice to her left. 'Oh, sorry Bernice, just talking to myself' she replied, feeling herself flush with a redness she hoped that would not be discovered. Bernice gave her a rather dirty look and continued with what she was doing. 'Piss off you stupid bitch' she thought. She continued with what she was doing, daydreaming - about him.

The following day she bumped into him again. He was just coming out of the garage, this time fully clothed, but with a spanner in a very dirty and greasy hand as he was attending to a broken down ambulance that had just been delivered by the breakdown company.

'Hello you' he smiled at her. 'Haven't seen you for a few days, you o.k?' 'Yes I am fine' she replied but knowing he hadn't seen her through no fault of her own as she had been constantly looking for him, even going out to her car in the car park pretending she had left something in it, hoping all the time he would be around, hoping even for another flat.
She had even considered purposely puncturing a tyre herself in the hope he would mend it and she would be able to spend some more time with him, spark up a conversation, in which he would ask her out.

'Erm, I was going to ask you' she coyly started. 'Is it, er, is it possible that, I, er, might have your telephone number, er, just in case, er, I have another problem?' she quickly spat out, feeling once again her cheeks flushing against her red hair.

'Another problem?' he curtly replied, smiling, teasingly. 'With your car?'

'Yes, yes, of course' she stammered. 'You never know, I might break down or something like that and I would rather you come and fix it - that's if you are able to and might not be busy doing something else'.

'Here', he winked at her. 'This is my mobile number. Ring me whenever you need me'. He passed her his number which he had quickly written down on a scrap piece of paper and smiled that smile, that gorgeous, sexy smile of his, those hypnotising eyes twinkling in the sun. She felt transfixed, like a fox would be when it stares into a car's headlights, unable to move, unable to do anything.

'Thank you. Hopefully I wont need it' she said and then wished she hadn't, she didn't mean that all, but the words just came out.

He looked at her. This redheaded lady in front of him and he thought how pretty she was. He studied her for a second or two whist thinking thoughts that would be best suited at another time, but he was interested in her. Interested in her enough to hope that she would call him.

'You call me, whenever you need me, for whatever reason' he said with a raised eyebrow and a nod of his head. 'I might just do that then' she teased back.

She turned to walk away when he spoke again. 'Hey, I give a very good service you know!' She looked back at him and approached him again, very slowly. 'Is that a car service?' she teasingly said. 'Well, of course', he replied smiling again. 'Whatever else did you think I meant'. She knew she had fallen into his trap and she felt horribly uncomfortable. He was playing games with her and they both knew it. She felt herself flush again. So she smiled, blinked and walked away muttering, 'shit, shit, shit' under her breath.

She had left work and collected the children from the childminder's house. On returning home she found that her husband was out and she was pleased.

After washing up the dinner things she settled the children into bed and read the usual bedtime stories.

He was still not in. She momentarily wondered where he was then dismissed him from her mind. She poured herself a very long glass of chilled white wine and turned the television on.

She had just settled down to the nine o'clock news when the telephone rang. She got up and went to the hall to answer it.

'Hello, 349932' she announced.

'Good evening madam, is that Stephanie Bower?' came the enquiring response.

'Yes?' she questioned.

'Its Sergeant Denver here from the Maddox police station, we have your husband here. He has been arrested over drink driving'.

She found herself gulp with absolute amazement. Whatever will he do next she wondered with completed disgust and frustration.

'Has he hurt anyone' she asked with interest only for a third party.

'No, mam, he was pulled over earlier this evening as the officer concerned believed that his driving was rather erratic. We will be keeping him in custody tonight and he should be released from the station in the morning' came the reply.

'Thanks' she muttered and she replaced the receiver with a frown of anger. 'Now I suppose you will lose your licence as well you stupid bastard' she spoke out loud.

She wanted to ring the mechanic more than ever now. She knew in her heart she shouldn't but what else was there, apart from the children. All she did was work and clean. She didn't love him anymore and tonight she hated him.

Morning came and she drove the children to school. She was not on duty today. After a quick visit to the local supermarket she returned to unpack the carrier bags and tidy the beds. He still wasn't home. Anyway she didn't really want to see him. She decided to shower, change her clothes, re-do the make up and go out.

She found herself driving towards work. She wanted to see 'him' again. She pulled up outside the car park to check if his car was there. It wasn't and her heart sank.

She drove off again in the direction of town. Downhearted now and totally deflated she decided to go and have a coffee in one of the local cafes along by the river. She parked in the local car park and walked towards Pinichi's, a favourite of hers.

She opened the door and walked to a table. As she sat down she heard a familiar voice behind her say 'hello you, what you doing here?'

She turned round surprised to see the mechanic sitting on the next table with an empty cup and a read newspaper alongside it.

'Hello' she beamed. 'I was just out and thought I would have a coffee, fancy one with me?'

He got up and came round to her side of the table placing his newspaper on it and sat down.

'That would be lovely, thanks' he smiled back at her.

'You not at work today?' she excitedly enquired.

'No, have today and tomorrow off - for a change' he answered.

'Have you any plans?' she continued in response.

'Actually I'm flat hunting. I'm moving out of the place I live at the moment and need somewhere to rent pretty quick. Have seen one and have a couple more now to see, fancy coming with me to check them out?'

She couldn't believe her luck. Here she was alone, miserable, bored and continually angry with her husband and now this. Perhaps there was a God! Her heart was skipping and she was aware that she had blushed. Being such a red head she hoped that it wouldn't be altogether noticeable and he hadn't been aware of it.

'Yes, I would like that very much' she said as she ordered two coffees and shifted position in her seat to be more comfortable.

They left the café fifteen minutes later as his next appointment was in twenty minutes. They drove in his car, a black Audi TT which accelerated away quickly and in the direction of the other side of the river.

The flat was lovely. It was on the first floor of a block of three and was very airy and bright. The previous occupants had vacated just a week before and it had been professionally cleaned to a standard which was extremely impressive.

The agent took them from the hall to the lounge and the kitchen and then from the bathroom to the bedroom. The apartment was painted throughout in magnolia and had matching cream carpets in every room apart from the kitchen which had laminated flooring. The kitchen cupboard fronts were also of a cream colour and everything seemed to match so perfectly within the whole property.

'What do you think?' he asked her quietly as they walked back through to the lounge. 'Should I take it? There's also an option to buy eventually if I like living here enough'.

'I don't know', she answered, embarrassed for a moment that he thought her views might count.

'It IS lovely' she said. 'Is it what you want?'

'I think so' he said and with that turned to the agent and advised that he would take it. He wanted to move in the following week.

On the way back to the car she was so engrossed in their conversation that she hadn't seen the car approaching and as she went to cross the road the driver had to swerve to avoid her. The mechanic grabbed her arm for safety and pulled her towards him. She found her face was inches from his and she took in a big breath of both thanks and of excitement.

For a couple of moments they stood like that, just staring at each other, the chemistry alive within them both being apparent to each other.

He slowly released his grip on her arm and said very amusingly and softly

'Do that again and you will be going to hospital in an ambulance not dispatching one!'
'Thank you', she muttered still staring at those eyes, the eyes that seemed so deep, like pools of hypnotism.

'Hey, come here' he said and put his arm gently around her waist to escort her across the road. She wanted to stay that way for eternity. She didn't ever want him to let go. He instinctively felt that she was happy for him to hold her and that told him the answer to the unasked question he had been secretly searching.

They got into his car and this time drove slower back to where she had told him her car was waiting.

'Would you like to help me move in?' he enquired of her as she opened the car door to leave him.

She looked back at him, unable to believe his request.

'Yes, of course, of course I would' she stammered, hoping that her eagerness and delight at his request couldn't be detected too much.

'I have all of next week off, hopefully they will let me move in at the beginning part of it. Whats your shifts next week?'

Amazed and laughing she replied, 'guess what? I have leave next week too!' And she left him there, in his car, smiling after her. As she got back into her car she knew that her smile was bigger than his and she didn't think she would ever stop smiling.

On her return from the school run with the children, her husband had returned. Slumped in the chair as usual and engrossed in the television.

The children had run in, as usual, happy to be home. Once emptying the biscuit tin they hurried into the computer room where they would remain until tea time. Oblivious to their father's presence, unaware of his present predicament and totally disinterested.

She entered the room where he was and studied him silently, watching his every move. He had taken the chair by the French window which overlooked the garden, the garden that she tended. The garden whose weeds were her responsibility along with the pruning, the trimming, the tending and of course the grass cutting. She shifted her position so he would not notice her silent observation, her watchful gaze.

How she hated him. How she so despised him now. He had ruined everything, taken her life and crushed it with his selfish self pity.

He had closed his eyes, the empty glass which had contained scotch just minutes earlier, still in his hand. His head had leant backwards and his mouth had started to open, getting wider, wider and wider. She waited for the snoring to start. Little snorts to begin and then gradual grunts becoming loud rasping thundering noises interrupted at time to time by pauses. Each time he paused she held her own breath, daring to hope that maybe he wouldn't take another, that it would be over and he would make life easier, for once, for her.

The empty glass had fallen softly onto the carpet beneath him. She once again held her breath for fear that he would subconsciously realise he was not holding it any longer. He grunted a couple of times and made a noise with his mouth which had become dry to the dehydration of his previous alcoholic consumption. He licked his lips and continued the snoring once more.

As she continued to watch this now overweight and unkempt man she found herself justifying her premeditated adulterous affair. An affair which she hoped would blossom into so much more. If only it could now. But now has no guarantees, now has no promise, now could be nothing more than a trick of the light that captivates and ensnares. Now is not the future, after all, because now is the present. Now is what she was living. And at this moment in time, now was a living hell.

She arose, indignant, and ignored him, carrying out her tasks of cleaning the lunch boxes and preparing the dinner for that night before getting ready for the night shift ahead of her.

Even though her marriage was crumbling away at the seams, she was now in a happy place and as long as those children were safe when she was away she really couldn't have cared less about what her husband did.

She changed into her green uniform and kissed the children goodbye. She turned to him before leaving the house just to impress that if he had to have a drink that he made sure the kids were in bed and asleep, the least he could do. She would still worry though. Worry that if one of them needed something in the night that he would be in no fit state to see to them. She worried that if one of them were ill, that they would have to attend to themselves as he would probably be unconscious. At least the two older ones had mobile phones. They knew that they could contact her at anytime when she wasnt there, if daddy was 'sleeping' and that she would return immediately if there was a crisis to attend to. At least they weren't babies. She had to work, she had to keep the roof over their heads.

The following week came although it seemed to take forever. She had seen him in the garage working but tried very hard not to bother him. She didn't want him to think that she was besotted by him. She decided she would wait for his phone call instead. And it came on the Tuesday morning at eleven.

'Hello you, I've got the keys, care to join me?' He asked.

'On my way' she happily answered and with that grabbed her bag and keys and flew out the house as if it were on fire. The drive to his flat seemed to take forever. Every set of traffic lights on the way was red and she seemed to get behind every driver that refused to drive faster than 30 mph at any time.

She pulled into the car park and checked her make up in the vanity mirror on the inside of the sun visor.

He was waiting for her in his hall of the flat now tenanted by him as she walked up the flight of stairs. He had a bottle of champagne in one hand and two flute shaped glasses in the other.

'Hello you, joining me for one of these?' he smiled at her. She almost melted under that gaze of his.

'OH, YES!' she said and she walked in as he closed the door behind her.
His furniture was already in the flat. There was already a washing machine, oven and fridge in the kitchen anyway.

The corner sofa was a deep blue leather one which matched the dark blue curtains at the windows. In the corner of the room was a 40" plasma screen on a glass table and some books on mini coopers along side it.

'You seem to have already moved in then' she said to him.

'Yes, actually moved in the furniture yesterday, but this will be my first official night here. Have a look around'.

She went into the bedroom. There was a huge king size bed with blue bedding and a huge mirror on the wall. There were still boxes dotted around containing mainly clothes but because there was just him and this was just a flat there didn't seem to be much need for anything else.

She felt him behind her.

'Here' he said and he passed her a glass now full of champagne. She sipped at it, nervously and he led her by the hand to the bed and they sat down. They both knew why she was there. They both knew the moment they had been waiting for had come.

He took the glass away from her and gently pulled her to him. Softly he kissed her lips and she closed her eyes to block out anything else that might have interrupted such a moment.

She had no hesitation whatsoever in what may follow.

At two thirty she dressed. Filled with such unremembered happiness, she opened the door to leave him. Gazing into his eyes just one more time before having to return to normality, to the school run, to the husband. She kissed him once more and turned into the communal hallway.

'Steph?' came a familiar voice from the side. She turned, slightly alarmed, someone knew her, someone had seen her.

'Candice!'

Her journey home to the house was a mixed bag of happiness and worry. She hadn't know Candice lived there in the block. What if Candice said something? Steph had politely smiled after nodding in acknowledgement and fleeing down the staircase knowing he was behind her, standing in his doorway, half naked at the door with Candice open mouthed and puzzled standing on the staircase, looking from Steph to the mechanic and then back again in questioning thought.

If Candice did reveal what she had seen it would be all over the Control room like fire. All gossip usually was. But then Candice would know that she had been the cause of such talk and Candice was nice, wasn't she?

She was unsure of whether to talk to Candice, to try to get her not to say anything when her mobile rang. She pulled over to the kerbside to answer it.

'Hello you' came the voice on the other end.

'Hello again' she smiled at his voice in response. 'Did you say anything to Candice, did she say anything to you?'

'No, babe. She just stood there in the hallway, gaping at me. Don't know if it was my biceps or the fact that I was near-on naked that caught her that way!'

'Oh stop it, did she say anything?'

'No. I just shut the door on her' he answered laughing.
'I'm glad you think it so funny' Steph replied. 'What are we going to do?'

'Nothing. All she saw was you coming out of my flat, that's all'.

'Apart from the fact that you had hardly any clothes on, and that I was with you!'

'Babe, stop worrying. Doubt if she'll say anything. Anyway, when you coming back?'

'Tomorrow?'

'See you at ten then?'

'Yes, I'll see you at ten, although I am going to be shitting myself that she'll see me there again'.

'Then we will have to be more careful won't we'.

She disconnected the call, started the engine and engaged first gear. Smiling all the way to the school, she didn't care if her husband was drunk again, she didn't care about him at all. All she knew is that for once she was happy and that she was falling in love with a complete stranger. It was a dangerous game, but at that moment in time, she didn't care.

Jonny

JONNY WAS GAY. HE HAD been a call operator for five years before moving onto dispatch. He had taken the news of Belinda's death badly and spent a lot of his time in quiet thought regarding it. She and he had been good friends and he missed her, desperately.

He waltzed in, as usual with a feminine grace, and took his position once the handover from the previous dispatcher was completed. Sitting there, signing on and nodding in acknowledgement to his co-workers he commenced his long twelve hour shift.

His life had been a turbulent one and he had known many sorrows, from that of disapproving parents once he had told them of his sexuality, to that of broken relationships.

He wished he could just find that special, right person, someone who he could share his life and his bed with. He frequented the gay nightclubs regularly and had picked up many lonesome characters along the way but no-one had met his expectations, many just wanting a good time and to enjoy helping him spend his hard earned cash.

Belinda was so special to him and he missed her. There wasn't a day that passed without him thinking of her and the times he had confided in her the problems he had.

When that email hit his screen that particular day he sobbed so much he had to be released from duties as he was totally inconsolable with grief.
But life had to go on, he knew that only too well from the job he did. Life was precious and life was all too very short.

This particular shift was proving to be a busy one, dispatching the resources, covering their places, watching for meal breaks, watching that he had adequate back-up so that when category A calls were logged by the call operators he had plenty of vehicles that could reach their destination with in the Government's appointed eight minute directive. He had to achieve, as the other dispatchers had, so that the figures looked good for the Government. The stress factor was extreme and they were all under immense pressure.

There was someone, however, that he had seen and rather fancied. To begin with it was hard to tell if the other person was interested but the more he saw him wandering around and the more he smiled at him when passing, the more the other guy smiled back, he thought he might have a chance.

However, tonight. he wouldn't be there. The other guy only worked during day light hours. Jonny tried not to let that get him down, after tonight he was off for a couple of days and then he would be back on the day time shifts. He would look forward to seeing him then, in the garage ...... where the mechanic worked.

Jonny, The Mechanic And Stephanie

THE GARAGE WAS ALWAYS A busy place, dirty but organised, a team of mechanics worked throughout each week day. There was of course only one that stood out.

Jonny decided to approach the mechanic that so interested him.

'Morning my love' he smiled as he waltzed into the large workshop.

'Oh, hello you!' came the response. 'What brings you in here, oh and watch out, you'll get dirty if you lean on that'.

Jonny instantly jumped backwards from leaning on a rusting exhaust pipe that had just been removed from an older ambulance and quickly brushed his leg with his beautifully manicured hand so that his uniform wouldn't be spoilt in any way. He was very particular about his appearance and hated to get dirty.

Jonny continued. 'Was wondering if you could look at my car sometime sweetie'.

'Yeah, sure, where is it and whats wrong with it?'

'Its that old mini over there, its making a strange noise and I was a bit worried that something might fall off'.

'Well, we don't want anything falling off, now do we?! I can look at it after work tonight. I am particularly good with minis, what time do you finish?'

'At seven, but if you cant fit it in I could always pop it round to you, where do you live by the way?'

'No, you're alright - I can see to it just past five when I finish. Give me the keys and I will check it out for you'.

Jonny handed over a set of keys with a pink key fob attached to them.

'Mind you look after it won't you, I have had it a long time and I love it to pieces. An old friend, Belinda, came with me when I got it and its very special to me. Don't get it dirty will you?!'

'Er, no, I will take good care of her'.

'Him'.

'Sorry, "him!"'

With that the mechanic put the keys in his pocket, watched carefully by Jonny, smiled and nodded his head as if in a farewell and carried on leaning over the inside of the bonnet of the first responder car he was attending to.

Jonny watched him silently for just a moment, his thoughts very much with this gorgeous man, and silently turned and walked away casting his head back in the direction of the garage once he returned to the Call Centre.

Throughout the day Jonny found it hard to concentrate, his thoughts elsewhere for most of the remainder of that shift. He continued to consider if the mechanic was straight or not. He certainly seemed friendly enough but it was too early to tell, he would have to work harder on him.

Five o'clock came and he observed the mechanic from the window attending to his beloved car he so cherished.

At twenty past five the mechanic signalled to Jonny to come over to the car park. Excusing himself with the supervisor Jonny left the building, his heart beating a little faster.

'Your car is fine, mate. The noise you could hear was a loose exhaust. I have tightened it up and you shouldn't have any more problems with it. Trouble is with these old cars, they are so low down that every speed bump you hit its going to cause you trouble. Try to slow down for them, eh?'

'Thank you' said Jonny, feeling a little flushed and wishing, even though the thought of any expense was not a nice one, that it could have been something a little worse.

'You know', said the mechanic, wiping his hands on some paper towel, 'I have some books at home on minis, I've had a couple of the old bangers in my time. You are welcome to have them if you like'.

Jonny couldn't believe his ears. He wasn't at all interested in any books on minis, but this guy was offering him something, maybe more?

'Oh, sweetie, that's kind of you. Shall I pop round and collect them at some stage, can I come tonight , where do you live?' Instantly he wished he hadn't opened his mouth and rushed out his requests, but it was too late, it had all been said.

Quite unexpectedly the mechanic agreed. 'Yeah, tonight should be alright. Come after work. 'I live the other side of the river, Cambrose Court - number 7'.

'Oh goodie, I will come straight from work then'.

'Yeah, alright then mate. See you later'. And he walked away not realising the implications of what was to follow.

The remainder of Jonny's shift seemed to take forever. It hadn't helped that for once the people in that particular part of the world seemed to all be well, no one had chest pain or difficulty in breathing, no one was crashing their car, no one was in labour and no one was feeling suicidal.

At last seven came. He checked his appearance again, and quickly rushed out to his car which was waiting for him in the car park, the exhaust this time secure and noise-less.

He drove swiftly over to the mechanic's flat which was easy to find on the other side of the river. Parking the car, he felt his heart skipping beats and he could feel a slight perspiration on his brow. He wished that he could have gone back to his home, where he lived with his mother, to shower and change, but no time. Not tonight.

He rang the doorbell and it was opened swiftly by the mechanic standing there bare chested, bare footed and wearing just a pair of white shorts. Jonny nearly fainted.

'Hello you, come in' was the greeting and the door was swung open for Jonny to make an entrance.

In the lounge were three Mini Cooper books, as promised. All in immaculate condition as was the interior of this gorgeous man's flat. An apartment that seemed to say batchelor but then there was something very feminine about it. Could it be that this man was gay too or was there a female influence about somewhere? He couldn't see any evidence to anyone else living at the flat, but there was just that 'something'.

'You'll have to excuse me, I have just got out of the bath' the mechanic apologised as he walked past, the smell of Ralph Loren's Polo almost visible in the air.

'Ok, dearie, no worries'. Shall I sit?'

'Yeah, you want a drink?'

'Ooh, what you offering?'

'Scotch, vodka, lager, wine?'

'Well then, how about a small glass of wine, have you any red?'

'Yeah, think I have a bottle of Merlot somewhere. Give me a minute'. And he disappeared out of the room to the kitchen to find the bottle that he knew was in the cupboard under the sink.

It was obvious to Jonny as the hour passed that if this guy was straight then he had no hang-ups whatsoever about being in Jonny's camp company. They seemed to get on really well, discussing the subject of minis and hardly spoke of anything else.

A second glass of red wine was poured and Jonny said it would have to be his last as he was having to drive.

Jonny didn't really know what to make of the situation. If he was gay then should Jonny approach him? But then if he was straight he would probably get his teeth knocked down his throat. But then again if he was gay and Jonny didn't approach him would he miss his chance. It was all so confusing, so annoyingly frustrating.

After another hour and a refusal of a third glass Jonny decided that the best course of action would be to leave and make an arrangement to see the mechanic again, that way if the mechanic wanted to make a move on him he would do so then and there. If not, it could wait for another day, why rush things anyway. He was still very uncertain which way this man swung.

'Anyway', Jonny started. 'I reckon I should go now. Thanks ever so for the books, that was so kind of you. Perhaps I could pop over again sometime?'

'Yeah, yeah of course, anytime you are passing. It was good of you to come all the way over here. We must do it again sometime' and the mechanic arose from the cross legged position he had been sitting in on the floor and approached the front door into the communal hallway.

'Er, shouldn't you put some clothes on, its getting rather chilly you know' Jonny worryingly fussed.

'No, I shall be fine' laughed the mechanic and opened the door.

Just at that split second he heard a rather familiar voice behind him from a girl carrying food in two carrier bags up the communal stairs to her own apartment.

'Jonny?'

Jonny turned. His mouth agape.

'Candice!'

He rushed down the flight of stairs towards the main entrance and fled to his car. A thousand thoughts flying through his mind. Candice, unexpectedly appearing, obviously living in the same block, seeing the two of them. The mechanic in his white shorts, Jonny leaving him half naked, what would Candice think and what would she say. Or would she say anything?

His journey home to his mother's house was a very hurried one. He just wanted to get home to collect his thoughts in the privacy of his home, where his mother would have cooked his tea and where he could escape to his room to collect this mixed bag of confusing thoughts.

He had got on so well with the mechanic. He had really had a great evening. He fancied him like mad, did the mechanic feel the same, could he be interested? Why did the mechanic invite him if he wasn't interested? Was he in a relationship? Was that feminine touch his or did it belong to a girlfriend, did he swing both ways? His thoughts went over and over in his head until he thought it would explode.

Full of his mother's home made lasagne and the two previous glasses of red wine, he laid on his bed and slowly drifted off to sleep without that shower or even cleaning his teeth.

The telephone rang at ten o'clock.

'Hi babe' she softly spoke. 'Can I come over tomorrow? Its Saturday, neither of us are working and the kids are out all day.

'Hello you, yeah, come over. I was just thinking of you. I've missed you' the mechanic replied.

'See you tomorrow then' she ended and replaced the receiver.

She parked her car two roads away. She didn't want Candice to see her again. She had checked the rota as, like her, Candice was also, annoyingly, off that day.

She rang his mobile to tell him she was just coming and to get the door open so that she could rush straight in.

He was waiting for her, in the bedroom, as he usually was.

Their affair had now been ongoing for three months and she had fallen hopelessly in love with this man. They never spoke of the future, just of the present. He knew she was unhappily married and had children. He also knew now that she was some years older than him, but neither of them cared. They just lived for the moment and enjoyed each other.

She had a shower and dressed. They chatted for a while and then it was time for her to go. Time to go back to normality again. She hated leaving and wished she could stay but there was no chance of that. She would never have left her children and the flat was too small for all of them. Besides, the future was never discussed and not wanting to spoil what they had, she left the future alone. For now. He, on the other hand, was happy for her to leave. He wasn't looking for any long term commitment, nor for any baggage.

She kissed him tenderly before making him check outside the door which he thought was hilarious and then she left, quickly and as silently as she arrived.

Walking towards where she had previously left her car, she didn't see the mini pulling up in the near distance or the driver in it. She continued with her head down so that she could escape without Candice spotting her again.

The driver of the mini stretched his long legs from out of his car. One day he must get a bigger vehicle he thought.

He crossed the road and approached the block of flats where the mechanic lived. He cleared his throat and hoped that if Candice was off that she wouldn't be in and hope that he would escape her noticing him. Once was bad but twice, in the same week would be suicide.

He rang the bell and could hear the voice of the mechanic behind the door.

'Just coming, hold on'.

The door opened. He stood there in a dressing gown, needing a shave but looking absolutely glowing. Jonny wondered if there was someone with him and felt a tinge of jealousy and disappointment at that thought. He also wondered what the mechanic may have been up to, at three in the afternoon, still undressed and looking like he had just got up.

'Hello you' said the mechanic. 'What brings you here?'

'Er, just passing. I thought I would return the compliment and bring you a bottle of wine'. He held up a bottle of shiraz which he had purposely just purchased from the local off licence.

'Oh, thanks' came the response. 'Er, do you want to come in then?'

'Might be an idea, or we could drink it out here of course lovie' came Jonny's sarcastic but witty response.

The mechanic allowed him in and closed the door silently behind him, neither of them not realising that Candice had actually been descending the communal stairs with the trash. She stood still for a moment then changed her mind, taking the rubbish back with her, nodding in silent disbelief all the while. Not only did Jonny and the mechanic not realise that she had seen Jonny and the wine entering the mechanic's flat but that also on cleaning her lounge window just fifteen minutes previously, she had noticed Stephanie leaving. 'Just what IS going on?' muttered Candice in puzzlement quietly to herself.

The mechanic went to the kitchen and returned with two glasses.

Jonny observed that there was an empty bottle of wine on the coffee table along with two used wine glasses which appeared to have been recently drunk from.

Somebody had been there before him and Jonny felt that tinge of jealously and disappointment surge over him again. Was his visitor male, or even worse, female?.

His chain of thought was disturbed when the mechanic spoke.

'You ok?'

'Yes, sweetie, I am fine' and he took the glass and watched while the mechanic slowly fondled the unopened bottle.

'So what brings you here then?' asked the mechanic with his searching hypnotic eyes.

'To be honest, I had a great time the other night chatting about my mini and your previous ones. Thought we got on well, so thought I'd just pass by with this bottle of wine, but I see you may have already had some before me' and he glanced at the two used glasses on the table and empty bottle of wine alongside it.

'Just a friend' smiled back the mechanic.

'So, shall we open this then?' Jonny enquired, hoping all the time that the mechanic, standing there in his dressing gown, had nothing on underneath and that perhaps his wildest fantasy might actually become reality sometime very soon.

The mechanic took the corkscrew, for the second time that day, and slowly proceeded to open the bottle.

After the first glass had been consumed Jonny plucked up the courage to ask his next question.

'So, what are you doing tonight then?'

'Well, I'm actually seeing an old friend' came the reply.

Jonny felt another surge of envy seep through his tall thin frame. He felt his face flush with an embarrassed look of disappointment. Maybe this 'friend' was really just and old friend, maybe someone he used to work with, someone he grew up with?

'Jonny?'

'Oh, sorry sweetie, just thinking. Look, I should really be going, I shouldn't be here wasting your time'.

The mechanic slowly observed him for a second or two then said 'you aren't wasting my time. Its nice that you felt you could come over. Look, if ever you want to discuss minis then just give me a call. Maybe we can get together at one of those mini rally functions sometime?'
Jonny was totally deflated. He should have known better. The mechanic wasn't interest in him. It was obvious that he saw them purely as friends and the sweet odour lingering obviously proved that his friends were of the female variety.

He rose to leave.

'Thanks for bringing the wine' the mechanic said.

'No trouble lovie, no trouble'.

He so wanted to just get out of that flat and escape down the staircase.

As they approached the door Jonny surveyed the mechanic once more. His muscle bound body fitting the dressing gown so well. For such a fine specimen of a man he was extraordinary gentle and he was calm, softly spoken and gallant.

The mechanic opened the door to the communal hallway.

'See you' he said and with that he winked at Jonny.

Was this for real or was this a game? Now Jonny was angry. He felt as if the mechanic was playing with him. The mechanic would know by the way Jonny was acting that Jonny was hoping his luck was in. This was just a cat and mouse game here.
'Bye' replied Jonny, And then he was gone.

He HAD to find out more. He had to find out who the visitor was that afternoon. Was this the one he was going to see that night or was it someone else? Was that friend really a friend just like he had said or was it more?

He wanted to return but he didn't want to scare the mechanic off. He decided to secretly return later and see where the mechanic went. He thought he would follow him. He needed to know if this old friend was male or female and if this friend was just a friend or something else? In which case maybe, just maybe, he, Jonny, might actually be in with a chance?

Night Time
Revelations

JONNY HAD SPENT THE NEXT few hours hiding in his car just down the road where he believed he had the perfect hiding spot and hoped that no-one could see him. His wait seemed to last for ages and although tired, especially after that glass of wine, he tried to concentrate and keep focused on what his goal of that night was.

He didn't have to wait for long. Just before the sun set and the darkness engulfed the area by the river the mechanic appeared. It seemed as if he was waiting for someone. Maybe a taxi? Suddenly a car drove up and the mechanic smiled and waved at its driver. The car seemed familiar and as Jonny was trying to establish where he knew the car from a very familiar person emerged from it.

The two bodies embraced each other and he took her face in his hands and kissed her lips. She responded with all the passion only two people very much in love would. They appeared to talk to each other briefly before he smilingly led her by the hand to the block of flats which he called home.

Jonny stared in absolute disbelief. Of all the people he didn't expect to see HER. He didn't expect the awaited friend to be such a 'good' friend. He wondered enviously how long it had been going on, after all they seemed to be pretty close.

She had certainly kept THAT quiet. He started the engine and pulled away, his disappointment turning into eager anticipation of being the bearer of the next piece of juicy gossip in the Control Room.

As he led her up the stairs, clean shaven and casually dressed, they heard footsteps emerging from the stairs above. She hoped that the footsteps did not belong to Candice but whoever it was they were to bump straight into each other before they could make his front door.

He looked at her in quiet confirmation that it didn't matter but as the footsteps approached her fears became reality.

Face to face she had to say something, after all she did work with her.

'Candice' she said.   'Er, hello'.   She tried to smile convincingly.

Candice, who was all ready for a night out and thinking of meeting friends at the old wine bar in the town, just stared. At first at her, then at him and then back to her.

And in quiet, puzzled astonishment before slowly passing by, she simply but politely replied 'evening .... Polly'.

Day Time Revelations

GRIFF WAS ALREADY SEATED AT his station, logged onto the system and was cracking his usual jokes with Stephanie who was sitting opposite him.

Jonny came bounding in, as usual slightly late.

'Hi guys' he sung out to a chorus of 'hellos'.

As he passed Griff heading towards the dispatch end of the control room he paused slightly and interrupted the laughter that was coming from Stephanie in response to Griff's last joke he had told her.

'Griff, what time is your break?   I have something to tell you that you'll never guess!'

'Ten - what is it?'

Both Griff and Stephanie looking at him in puzzled yet eager anticipation.

'Wait and see! I'll see you at ten, the sergeant major is looking at me'. And he fled into the direction of Bernice and the dispatchers.

Ten came and Griff was waiting for Jonny in the foyer.

'Come on then, whats it all about?' Griff was so dying to know the next piece of juicy gossip from his informant.

As they walked towards the canteen they were joined by Stephanie, who by this time was looking rather ill.

'You alright Steph?' enquired Griff.

'Yes, keep feeling sick' she replied and as they approached the doors of the canteen she fled to the ladies loos.

Griff and Jonny sat down after collecting their coffee.

'Guess who is having an affair with that gorgeous hunk of a mechanic?' Jonny proudly announced. Excitedly awaiting the response from his friend.

'Go on then, who is it?' Griff really wasn't very interested. He didn't know the mechanic and he was a little disappointed that this was the big news of the day. He thought Jonny was going to reveal something much better. Until the bombshell was dropped of course.

'Polly'.

'POLLY?'

'Yep, Polly!'

'Polly?' Griff asked again. His heart now feeling as if it were in his boots, for Polly was the girl he so fancied himself.

'How do you know?' Griff enquired, hoping that perhaps Jonny had got it all wrong. It wasn't the first time for Jonny was a well known gossip and loved to exaggerate everything, probably because his own personal life was so boring and he obviously had nothing better to do than make trouble for other people.

'I saw them - together! They looked very much the loving couple to me'.

'You SAW them? Where?' What were they doing then?'

Griff was determined to find out, to confirm whether he stood any kind of chance with the girl of his dreams.

'I was outside his flat, been in there for a drink, and saw them. She got out her car and they kissed and everything. Then he took her inside'

'How come you know where he lives then, how come you were there, eh?'

'I've been over there a loads of times' Jonny exaggerated. 'As I was leaving I saw them, couldn't keep their hands off each other'.

'Blimey Jonny, you sure?'

'Yep, sure as eggs are eggs sweetie, sure as eggs are eggs'.

'Shit'.

Stephanie emerged from the ladies still looking pale and walked towards them, weaving in and out of the next course of people taking their paramedic exam and heading towards the direction of reception.

'Best not to tell Steph' Griff said. 'We don't want this to get round and she doesn't look well either'.

The reality was that Griff didn't want anyone to know at all. He wanted Polly to himself and wanted everyone else to know that she could be his, and not belong to someone else, especially that distinguished, suave and smooth talking knob of a mechanic. How he hated him right now. He would have to catch up with Polly and find out for himself. It was feasible that Jonny had got it all wrong. And just why was Jonny round his place anyway. He would have to find out.

Stephanie returned to the table, went to sit down and promptly fainted instead.

'Bloody hell' said Jonny as he rose to attend to her. 'Better get some help here'.

The ambulance was called from the control room and arrived promptly. Even though this was H.Q. there were usually no available ambulances as each one was either on cover or at a station. Luckily 'Delta 1471' was close by.

She was taken to hospital and was the talk of the control room, Jonny's news remaining, for now, a secret between both him and Griff.

—

Delta 1471 handed over their patient to the nursing staff and left for their next patient. She had recovered instantly in the canteen but upon advice of the crew she agreed to go to St Margaret's hospital just to be checked over.

She had been feeling so unwell these past few weeks. She couldn't keep anything down and was constantly tired.

A doctor saw her within a short while and took her history. Her blood pressure was higher than it should be and he arranged for some blood tests, agreeing that she could be discharged as long as she went home to rest, and urged her to contact her doctor for the results in a few days.

—

Candice had started her shift at seven that evening. Mike had winked at her on his way out of his office and she smiled inwardly, longing to be with him again. He had told the 'old crab' that there was a Managers Conference that coming weekend and he was going to be away from Friday until Sunday night. Of course there was no conference at all. Instead he had got tickets to Paris for the weekend and was taking Candice with him. She was already packed, not that she needed much as they would not been venturing out of the hotel bedroom for the two days they would be there.

She had already decided to inform Mike about his daughter. He would not like the news very much as he had big plans for Polly. The thought of his little princess with that mechanic would not be accepted well. After all he was obviously much older than her for a start and added to that was the fact that he was obviously playing about. Having witnessed the comings and goings in that flat of his, goodness knows what was going on.

He had reacted very badly about his little princess getting drunk 'that' night, especially in her care, but then she had retaliated in the fact that he had kept Polly quiet from her.

She also realised that gossip spread very quickly in the Control Room, like all establishments, and if Mike had heard the news from some other source he would be fuming, especially as Candice knew and hadn't filled him in first.

Even though she was such good friends with Polly, she couldn't let Polly know HER secret so she couldn't say anything to her. Polly had kept a distance from Candice since that night, the night she was seen with the mechanic. And Candice was pleased, pleased that she hadn't been in the position of having to discuss what she witnessed.

No, there was no doubt. She must tell him and the sooner the better.

———

Stephanie picked up the telephone as soon as her husband had left for his local liquid lunch down the pub.

She dialled the number and waited anxiously for the receptionist to connect her to where she would get the results of her blood tests.

As she sat patiently waiting, drumming her finger nails on the breakfast bar where she sat, watching the steam coming from her newly made fresh cup of coffee and considering the pile of washing and ironing that lay ahead of her for that day, a voice answered.

'Hello, yes we have your results back' came the voice. All of a sudden Stephanie was engulfed with the dread that something terrible was going to be revealed. Did she have some form of cancer, was she going to battle with it same way that Belinda did? Was it some other kind of dreadful disease, was she terminally ill?

The longed for news was about to be revealed.

The female voice on the other end of the phone seemed friendly but professional. She knew what was wrong and was about to deliver Stephanie's prognosis.

'The results show that you are pregnant'.

The female voice continued and was saying something else but Stephanie wasn't listening. The words 'pregnant' going continually round and round in her head 'pregnant, pregnant, pregnant, pregnant, pregnant'.

Reeling from the news she had just received she realised she was still holding the receiver, tightly, in her hand. She replaced it gently, quietly, as if it was so fragile it would break at the slightest touch. Palms sweating, she brush the hair from her face backwards and stared at the empty space ahead of her in silent disbelief, unable to get to grips with the news that had just been handed to her.

She stretch out for her mobile. She dialled the familiar number, desperate to hear his voice, needing to see him, to be with him, all the more than ever.

The ringing seemed to continue forever when suddenly the call was answered.

'I need to see you' she whispered.

'Now?' came the one answered reply.

'Yes, its urgent. Can I come over now?'.

There was a pause and then a sigh from the other end.

'Its not that convenient at the moment' he replied. 'Cant it wait?'

'No, I need to see you now. I need to talk to you about something'.

'O.k. but not now. Give me a couple of hours'.

And then the line was cut. She didn't even think about questioning why she would have to wait. She didn't even think about why he couldn't see her immediately. All her thoughts were concentrating on the news that had jut been delivered and the terrible mess that was about to unfold.

She sat, silently, staring into the deep dark empty void ahead of her. In the distance a siren was wailing on its way to or from another emergency, a dog was barking and a car alarm had suddenly been activated, but she didn't hear any of it. She was just staring, oblivious to everything and now, afraid.

An hour had elapsed since her conversation with him. It seemed like a week. No longer could she just sit there, she knew she had to go to him and she knew she had to do it now.

She grabbed her bag and threw in her phone. Picking up her keys she swiftly walked her way to the door and to her car which would take her to him.

—

Jonny had taken a chance. He had known the mechanic was home and, impulsively as ever, he knew that there was no time like the present to make a move, his move. He had to know, one way or another and he wasn't prepared to wait any longer.

He knocked gently on the door preferring that to ringing the bell. There was no answer. Tiny beads of perspiration appeared on his forehead. He knocked again, this time a little louder.

He heard the footsteps approach and Jonny felt his heart beating faster and faster. The door opened and the mechanic stood there.

'Hello you, what brings you here' he said with a smile so inviting, so teasing it made Jonny think that his heart was going to explode.

Jonny mustered up the courage he knew he would need and continued with his prepared speech that he had practised over and over again in his head.

'Can I come in? I wasn't passing this time. I intended to come by!'

The mechanic opened the door and gestured him in with a mock form of a royal beckoning. He had opened the door wide enough for Jonny to just brush past him, their two bodies making contact. Jonny could feel himself blushing.

'So', the mechanic continued as he indicated for Jonny to enter the lounge and sit on the sofa. 'Tell me why you are here then'.

Jonny knew this was his chance. He hated suspense and was the sort of person who just lived for today and forget the consequences. He had nothing to lose and if his suspicions were right then he was in the right place. He took a long deep breath.

'I suspect' he started, staring at the floor, 'I suspect you might be the same as me. I had a feeling from the first moment I came here'. He glanced up at the mechanic who was still standing in front of him.

This is it, thought Jonny. Any minute now he is going to throw me out.

He quickly looked away from the mechanic's glaze and studied the floor a little longer, the pause long and atmosphere in the air feeling cold.

The phone started to ring and the mechanic excused himself to answer it, walking away whilst talking softly, out of earshot down the receiver. After a moment or two, he returned to the room.

'Erm' the mechanic started. 'Can you clarify, perhaps?' The mechanic was smirking. He knew what Jonny was trying to do but wanted to play with him a little longer, like a cat does with a mouse before going in for the kill,

Jonny felt a little mocked. He knew was playing with him. He continued.

'I, er, I don't want to beat about the bush, if you know what I mean. I had a feeling from day one that we might, er, might be a little, er, more than, er …'

'Oh, for God's sake man, get on with it'

'Friends?'

Jonny glanced over to the mechanic.

'Friends? What kind of, "er … friends" then?'

Jonny froze. It had been a mistake. The speech he had so well rehearsed in his mind had crumbled away. He couldn't remember any of it. And he was fidgeting. He wanted to run now to get away, wishing with all his heart he hadn't done this stupid thing. Of course the mechanic wasn't up for grabs. He should have known that. And more than that, he was obviously straight.

He got up to leave.

The mechanic grabbed his arm.

That's it, thought Jonny. Goodbye teeth.

'Where you going?' the mechanic asked with a suggestive upward turn of his mouth. 'Don't you want to stay - to find out?'

Jonny swallowed hard. Oh my God, he thought.

The mechanic slowly released his grip on Jonny's arm but didn't let go.

'Come on, then' he said, softly, almost hardly sounding at all. 'The bedroom's this way'.

Jonny thought he was, for just a second, going to die, right there on the spot.

'Really?!' came the stupid reply. Jonny was starting to regret being there. He wanted to seduce the mechanic, more than that, he wanted the mechanic to seduce him. He had dreamt it every single night since the first meeting. Why oh why did he say 'really' of all things.

'Yes, come on'.

And the mechanic led him by the arm to the bedroom, and quietly closed the door.

—··—

She didn't know how she got there. The drive was a complete blur and she was totally oblivious to anything around her. She just knew she had to get to him, to see him, to be with him and in his arms once again.

As she pulled up alongside the roadway she glanced around her, as usual, checking that the coast was clear. She didn't see the mini parked just two cars in front.

She opened the car door, grabbing her bag in the process and locked her vehicle up. Quickly she made her way to his door, lightly treading the steps towards it.

'Hurry, hurry' she whispered as she rang the door bell. He seemed to take forever in coming to let her in.

Eventually she heard his footsteps and then the door opened. He stood there, looking dishevelled, and he was wearing very little. He seemed a little shocked at seeing her there even though he knew should would be coming.

'I thought you were coming later' he silently spoke through the half opened door that she expected him to have opened for her.

'I couldn't wait, I need to talk to you … are you going to let me in?' her tone was quiet as she was petrified that Candice may, as ever, appear like magic. She looked at him in slight frustration that her greeting was not as she expected and in that he hadn't welcomed her as he would usually have done. She hadn't noticed he was half naked.

She pushed past him with no warning, as he closed the front door, and made her way into the lounge. He followed and closed the lounge door behind him.

'I need a drink' she said as she turned to face him. It was more of a statement than a request.

Before he could answer she heard the sound of the front door quietly closing. Puzzled she glanced in the direction of the noise. 'What was that?' She strained her neck past his body which had now stood between her and the lounge door, as if she would see someone appear, expecting someone to open the door and walk in to join them.

In fact no-one would appear, as the visitor who had been there had now discretely left in the hope that she would not even notice.

She glanced back at the mechanic, frowning a questioning look without speaking. He just stared back at her, his face slightly flushed and now, something she had never seen, a nervous look about it.

'There's no-one there' he said'.

'But I heard the door' she replied in slight annoyance and in a concerned tone. 'And just how can you know there's no-one there when you haven't even gone and checked?' Her voice was now becoming slightly louder and firmer.

She stared at him for a few seconds and realised he was not going to look, not even going to check. She knew he had closed the front door behind him when she arrived so it couldn't have blown shut. Her heart started to beat louder, she was now becoming frightened and suspicious.

She brushed past him, too quickly for him to stop her. She entered the hall. There was no-one there and the front door was shut. She turned to the bedroom door. It was open, but she was sure that it was shut when she came in.

She pushed open the bedroom door. The bed was unmade, ruffled. She slowly walked towards it, swallowing, hoping that the doubts entering her mind were unjust.

She grabbed the corner of the duvet and pulled it back. The bed was warm.

He had followed her, helpless to do much else. She felt his stare on the back of her head and she turned to face him, the reason her being there then far from her thoughts.

Trying hard not to show any form of emotion but unable to hold back the tears that had formed in her eyes and now sat on the edge of her bottom eyelids ready to make their descent down her cheeks she looked him up and down. At that moment she realised he was dressed in nothing but silk boxer shorts. The boxer shorts she had bought him.

'Who's been here?' There was silence in response and he did nothing but just stare at her, not knowing what to say.

'I said who's been here?' This time her voice was raised, louder than usual and slightly on the borders of hysterical. Once again he said nothing.

'Look .... I ....'

'No' she said. 'Don't explain. Your silence told me everything'.

She pushed by him, entered the lounge to take her bag, before leaving. As she opened the front door she turned slowly to look at him. He was still standing there in the entrance of the bedroom, his back towards her. She went to say something, to ask who she was, but decided better of it and slammed the door, hard, behind her.

She rushed down the communal stairs and, once again, walked straight into the obvious neighbour who always had the knack of just being there, always it seemed.

Briefly they stared at each other. Candice looked at her in quiet amusement.

'Hi' is all she said as Stephanie marched past with a tearstained face.

'Bollocks' was the reply.

—

Jonny had driven fast back to the house he lived at with his mother. He had a wide grin on his face and, although his very successful and amazingly unexpected day had been cut disappointedly, prematurely short, he was ecstatically happy. He had got what he wanted and hoped there would be more, much more.

However he was puzzled about the interruption. Hushed voices, closing of doors. He knew it would be best to make a silent retreat.

There would be more of what he had had to come in the future, he just knew it. But what was she doing there. He was sure he knew the voice, he had heard it so often at work. But he couldn't be interested in her, not after he had just had him? No, he would have to warn her off. He would have to tell her she had no chance. She would get over it, move on and find someone her own age.

He made his mind up to tell her so at the retirement party being held for Joe Simmonds, a paramedic with twenty years service, the following week. Then if she left the picture the mechanic would be all his, after all she was obviously making a nuisance of herself, he remembered seeing her turn up at the mechanic's flat before. Yes, he'll tell her to keep her hands off. He had made up his mind to speak to Polly then.

Bernice

THE CALL CAME THROUGH THAT day at ten minutes past ten.

Bernice had been called into Mike's office and was told to close the door behind her. Concerned that she was about to get a reprimand for something, although not knowing what, she closed the door as instructed and sat down.

'I have just had a call from H.R. They say that they have received news that your mother has been seriously involved in a road traffic accident'. He carried on gently. 'I am sorry Bernice, there's no easy way to say this, but your mother has died. Your aunt has been trying to phone you at home but because you are obviously here and she didn't know how otherwise best to contact you she rang here. Bernice, obviously under the circumstances you will want to go immediately to the airport and fly over to America to be with her'.

Bernice showed no emotion. She was a very cold and hard faced woman, who felt very little of anyone but herself. However, this was her mother and even though as a child her mother had deserted her to emigrate to the U.S with the man she had left Bernice's late father for, she still felt that she should go to pay her 'last respects'.

'Yes, of course. Thanks Mike. Can I leave now and make some arrangements?'

'It goes without saying. I am sorry for your loss, Bernice' he quietly and softly said.
Bernice went straight home without saying anything to anyone. She telephoned the airport and was able to get a flight that evening. She packed a few things and rang Griff on his mobile. She knew that as Griff's father owned a taxi company, he was the best port of call.

'Griff, do you think you could give me the number of your father's cab company? I need to go to the airport tonight as my mother has unexpectedly and rather inconveniently died'.

'Oh, shit, Bernice I am sorry'.

'No worries, she was always causing chaos in my life, even in her death she continues to do so, but thanks anyway'.

'Look, I'm a bit short of cash myself and I'm off tonight. How about you give me, say £20 and I'll drive you?'

'O.K, whatever. Can you pick me up at 7? My address is 17 Portland Drive'.

'Yeah, see you then' he said and replaced his mobile in his pocket, delighted that he was going to earn some extra cash.

While she waited for the time to tick by she couldn't help but reflect on her childhood. She remembered how cold and unloving her mother was. Being an only child it should have been different, she should have been the centre of attention, the one who counted, but she was always having to bear the brunt of her mother's explosive behaviour.

She had been constantly told that she wasn't wanted, that she was a 'mistake', that it was her fault that her parents marriage wasn't perfect. 'Ever since you were born, you have been trouble' her mother would often say, and 'I wish you hadn't been born' was another saying her mother had been fond of.

Her father, a shy quiet little man, had died some years previously and Bernice had been distraught. She adored him and at times in adulthood often wondered if the special father-daughter relationship they shared was what was the cause of her mother's dislike of her.

He had a poorly paid job and money was tight but he did his best and she loved him. No one would ever come close to him, no one would ever match his standards. So she never tried finding a man of her own whom she could love and care for and who could love and care for her.

And here she was contemplating a funeral. Again. She telephoned her aunt to say she was going to fly out and to make arrangements in America for her accommodation.

Griff promptly arrived at seven. He carried her bag to the car, put it in the boot and opened the back door for her to get in but she ignored him and opened the front door instead. He, rather bemused, shut the rear door and got in the front with her, behind the wheel, starting the engine to drive them the twenty minutes to the airport which was done in total silence. Griff not wanting to say anything that might send Bernice into any emotional state, not knowing that Bernice actually despised this woman who had had the cheek to call herself a mother, and Bernice sitting there hoping that Griff wouldn't start reeling off any of his cheesy jokes in an attempt to try and make her laugh.

Laughing wasn't one of Bernice's good points. The rather large chip on her shoulder sat there permanently.

'Miserable old bitch' thought Griff as they continued up the motorway.

'Rotten stinking bastard' thought Bernice as she peered out of the passenger car window, wrinkling her nose up at a silent, fowl smelling fart that Griff had just passed.

Eventually, and with relief for them both, they drove up to the drop off point and he emerged from the car to open the boot where her bag lay in wait.

She handed him the £20 and nodded in quiet appreciation then she walked away in the direction of the main doors where, hopefully, thought Griff, she wouldn't ever come back out of.

He lit a cigarette and was just about to climb back into the driver's seat where, in the distance, he saw what he thought was Mike.

How strange, he thought. Mike could have taken the old cow, instead of me. And just where was he going anyway?

As he got into the car he observed Mike stop, as if he were waiting for someone. Griff decided he would stay put and wait himself. What was going on? Why was Mike at the airport too, and just who was he waiting for?

Just then, a black taxi cab drew up, in front of Griff. 'Typical' get in my view why don't you' he quietly spoke out loud.

The beautiful girl who climbed out was none other than Candice herself. She looked over to the main doors of the airport and waved. Oblivious to anyone or anything else.

'Jesus'. Griff said out loud as the penny dropped. 'Candice and MIKE?'.

He watched them embrace together while the black cab pulled out from the bay it had occupied whilst dropping off its passenger.

A policeman approached Griff to beckon him off as Griff was still stationary. Griff nodded in acknowledgement to the officer and drove very slowly away, watching the couple in his rear view mirror kissing each other, each with a small bag and obviously about to embark on a journey - together.

'Well, well, well' he thought as he accelerated away in the direction of the motorway. 'I must pop into Control to check how long Candice is off for. How interesting' and he quietly smiled to himself all the way back to the control room to check a few facts before putting his very clever plan into action.

———

Just as expected, Candice was booked off for the weekend, retuning for a Monday day shift and, being a manager, Mike would be out of the office until then too.

'Looks like I might just be in for a spot of promotion' Griff thought to himself as he left the building and got once more into his car.

Confrontation

MONDAY CAME. GRIFF HAD BEEN nervous all weekend, rehearsing what he would say over and over again.

He showered and dressed, admiring his reflection in the mirror as he carefully gelled back his hair. 'You'll do' he said to himself as he glanced one last time at himself and left for his journey to work.

He parked in his usual place and made his way to the control room, ready not just for his twelve hour shift which lay before him but also for a very important meeting which he decided he would insist upon as soon as Mike arrived.

At nine sharp Mike walked into the office.

As soon as he entered his office, Griff logged off the system and approached Mike's door.

Mike was just taking off his jacket to place it on the hook when Griff knocked on the door.

'Mike', started Griff. 'I need to see you, rather urgently'.

'I'm afraid it will have to wait Griff. I have certain things that need attending to and .....' He didn't get any further before Griff interrupted him. 'I am sorry Mike but this can't and won't wait. It's a matter of urgency, erm a matter of a little trip you took before the weekend'.

Mike looked at him, slightly confused and a little concerned. What did he know? What did he mean?

'Why don't you shut the door Griff. Mike indicated towards the door that was slightly ajar. He didn't know what Griff was about to say or indeed what his intentions were but he certainly didn't want any of the control staff overhearing.

Griff closed the closed and pulled up a chair. He sat down, without being asked to, and smiled rather sarcastically towards the manager.

Mike sat down too and turned towards him.

'Griff, I really have got a busy schedule today. If this can wait then perhaps you could come back about three or even ....'

Once again he was interrupted by Griff.

'No, now is fine. I am sure your appointments can wait a little while'.

Mike surveyed this rather young, cocky member of staff. He looked at him with an increasing amount of concern. He had mentioned his trip. How did he know about that? What did he know?

He was about to find out.

'As you know, Mike, I would like to be placed on the management course. As you also know, there is only one position available. I know there are several others that have indicated their interest, amongst whom is Bernice. However I think I should be the one who gets the place'.

'Griff, you haven't been here very long. The position is open to all those with certain standards, certain criteria, one of which is a lengthy time of service here. I can't possibly put your name forward .....'

Once again Griff cut in.

'Did you have a good weekend Mike?' Griff went in for the kill, his well rehearsed words flowing as if they were written out in front of him like a presenter on television would read an autocue.

'What do you mean?' Mike started to loosen the tie around his neck which had started to become slightly uncomfortable at this stage.

'I saw you. You and a certain other member of staff'.

'You saw me, where, when, what are you talking about?' Mike was becoming annoyed now but more than that he was inwardly becoming very uneasy. If his adultery was discovered he would be finished. His marriage would be over, his career would be in tatters, his life would certainly never be the same again.

'Lets not mess around here Mike. I saw you, at the airport'.

The telephone on the desk rang making Mike jump. He turned instinctively the answer it.

'Hello.......... Yes, I am just coming, sorry. I will be with you in five minutes'.

He replaced the receiver and turned to Griff again. His brow was hot and he felt sick.

'I need to go to a meeting. I have no choice. You will have to come back whether you or I like it'. He got up to take his jacket off the hook. Griff remained seated.

'O.k' said Griff, silently grinning inwardly. 'I will come back. I will see you at three then'. And he arose from his chair, opened the door and continued to his seat to log back in so he could continue to take the incoming calls, as if nothing had just happened, knowing that his plan was coming together very nicely.

Mike cleared his throat, and proceeded to his meeting which he was now late for.

Blackmail

MIKE'S DAY WAS GOING FROM bad to worse. His meeting with the Directors was not a very positive one and they were placing increasing high amounts of pressure upon Mike and his department for seemingly unobtainable targets.

He found himself unable to concentrate and found himself glancing at the huge wall clock which was placed in front if him where he had sat. The time ticked by agonising slowly and at one stage he almost believed the clock may have had something wrong with it. Checking his Rolex on several occasions he was relieved when at last the meeting concluded and he was able to return to his office.

Constantly during the previous hours he had been trying to take Griff's words into perspective. Over and over in his head he recalled Griff's words and tried to make sense of them all. What if he had been seen? So what. There was no proof. It was his word against Griff's. Candice for one would certainly deny anything. No, he had nothing to worry about.

The control room was, as always, busy and stressful. Operators talking, asking numerous questions, triaging calls, dispatchers allocating vehicles, sending units, covering resource points. He glanced over to where Griff was. Griff was seated at his station and looking back in Mike's direction, waiting.

He logged off once more and rose from his position.

'Just where do you think you are going?' Bernice demanded of him from across the desk. She was, as usual, her very normal, happy and polite self.

'Bernice' replied Griff, quietly and calmly, 'into Mike's office, not that it is ANY of your business. So if you don't mind ...' and he casually strolled into the managers office with a very indignant and furious supervisor left open mouthed behind him.

'Shut the door' Mike said without even looking round at him. He knew he was coming, he saw him rise from his seat as he entered the control room. He knew this was it and he was ready for any accusations. He was also ready for his denial.

Griff did as he was instructed and sat down on the same chair he had sat on previously, once again not waiting to be asked. He crossed his legs and leaned back comfortably.

Mike had taken his jacket off again and this time loosened his tie in preparation for what Griff was about to reveal.

'So', started Griff. 'As I was saying earlier. There is this position on the management course. I would like the place, please'.

He spoke politely, as if he was ordering from a menu, not waiting to be told that his selection was 'off' or that his choice of wine would not suit his main course. His tone was more of a statement, an order.

'As I said to you before Griff, there is no way you can have a place. Bernice is next in line and she has waited a very long time, the panel .....' Griff stopped him by putting his right hand up and indicating that he should stop speaking.

'Mike, I don't care about Bernice. I don't care whether she has waited a long time, she can wait forever for all I care. She will not get the place, I will'.

'How dare you speak to me like that, just who do you think you are'. Mike's voice became raised, angry. He felt himself losing control of this so-called meeting Griff wanted.

'Lets put it another way, shall we Mike?' Griff was now purposely becoming very irritatingly patronising.

He leant forward slightly. Steadily, calmly and softly he spoke. 'I WILL get this place on the course. I WILL become part of the management team. There WILL be no other competition. In return, Mike, I will keep quiet about your obvious affair with Candice. I will not speak of it to another living sole, including your wife'.

Mike had gone red in the face with seething anger.

'I don't know what you are talking about'.

'Oh, but I think you do, Mike. I think you know very much what I am talking about. But, whether you will take a chance and call my bluff is another thing. You have a lot at stake from my research. Shame to spoil it all, especially with just some young and pretty blonde call op. Bet she's good in bed Mike.'

'Get out'. Mike gritted his teeth and pointed towards the door.

'I take it that you will think about it then? I see by the rota that you AND Candice are both in tomorrow. So, I will come back in the morning, say nine again, and catch you again, for your answer which, as I am sure you will agree once you have slept on it, will be very favourable towards me indeed. In fact, very favourable for us both'.

Griff stood up, smoothed his trousers down and promptly left Mike's office, door ajar.

Bernice was straight in there.

'Mike, I have to talk to you about Griff. He is the rudest .....' She didn't get to finish her sentence or her grievance.

'Bernice, go away. Come back another time' is all the answer she received.

Shocked and surprised by Mike's attitude, she left as quickly as she came in. Griff was looking at her, smirking and thinking how she would react when she heard the news that she has lost the place to him. He decided to celebrate early and arrange to meet his friends down the pub later.

The Party

JOE WAS A REALLY WELL liked paramedic. So many people had turned out for his retirement party, even Rob had been invited as he and Belinda had spent many dinner parties with him and his wife when Belinda was alive.

The evening was progressing well. Joe had hired out the function room at the golf course and it was adorned with gold and silver helium balloons. Music was playing in the background and champagne and wine was flowing. The caterers had served up a remarkable finger buffet and people were arriving and greeting each other warmly.

Not everyone who was invited from the Service could attend, shifts had to be covered whether it was operational or control staff. But everyone who could attend did so.

Arriving slightly ahead of Mike and the old crab, Candice made a graceful entrance. She had her hair perfectly pinned up and wore a very low cut and short royal blue cocktail dress. She looked even more stunning than usual and some of the male guests were unable to cast their eyes away from her. She had arrived at the same time as Stephanie, Griff and Jonny, the latter of the two sharing a cab.

The mechanics who worked in the garage had also been invited. Jonny was eager to see if they showed up. He was only interested in seeing one of course and was constantly checking and re-checking the door to see if he would turn up.

He was also looking for Polly. He wanted her out of the picture and was going to make sure she stayed out of it. He wasn't sure how, or what he might even say to her, but he knew he had to get rid of her somehow. He wondered if she knew about the mechanic's games. He wondered if she realised that she was not the only lover in his life.

He decided to get a drink. For courage.

Mike and the old crab greeted Joe and were engrossed in conversation. He looked tired, drawn and somehow looked slightly older these past days. His heavily made up wife, dressed in another of her designer outfits which couldn't do anything to hide her aging skin, was laughing at something Joe had said and knocking back another glass of champagne as Bernice, dressed in a long sleeved and remarkably outdated evening gown, made her entrance with one of the dispatchers also invited.

Polly, who had been issued strict instructions from her parents not to touch a drop of alcohol, had appeared out of nowhere and had made her way over to Griff and Jonny who were chatting to Stephanie, who was knocking back a glass of wine.

Some of the guests had started dancing and choruses of laughter could be heard over party talk. It seemed that everyone was enjoying themselves, even though some, unbeknown to others, had worrying thoughts on their minds.

At ten o'clock Mike decided to give his speech which had been carefully prepared by himself in which he would formally say goodbye and good luck to Joe.

The lights had been made brighter for him and the music had been turned off so he could speak.

As he was at the part where Joe had served such a long time in employment, the door had opened and the mechanic silently walked in, hoping that he would not disturb the speech. Some didn't even notice him but under the watchful unnoticed eye of Candice, a rather inebriated Stephanie did. Jonny was overjoyed to have noticed him too. Polly also saw him.

'This might be interesting' thought Candice.

The speech continued …..

'And of course it goes without saying that after so many years of dedicated service you will be sorely missed Joe.

You are everyone's favourite paramedic, Joe. Everyone loves you and loves working alongside you. You make our job of caring for the community, caring for those that are sick, dying and comforting those around them so much better.

So, everyone, please raise your glasses to Joe'.

With that an huge round of applause was heard and jeers of 'Joe, Joe, Joe' in a prompt to take him to the front and replace Mike to return a speech.

Giving his glass to his wife and smiling he stepped forward to take his place.

As he spoke there were others at the function that weren't listening. These others had their own words to be said, quietly and out of earshot, to other members of the party.

Rob, who had arrived earlier, was chatting quietly to Stephanie in a corner of the room. They were engrossed in their own conversation, unable to be overheard and looking serious.

Candice glanced over trying to catch Rob's eye so that she could wave in a silent greeting, glad he had turned up, so pleased he felt he could face the world once more after Belinda's death.

She noticed how he seemed to be concentrating on every one of Stephanie's words and thought that he was probably trying to make sense of her slurred speech after too much alcohol.

She glanced over in the opposite direction of Mike and the old crab. Both were still listening, intently, to Joe's return speech. She surveyed his wife once more. This was, after all, only the second time she had been so close to her.

What did he see in her? What was it that kept him with her, Polly or the money? Or was it both? She looked over to where Polly was standing, her smile so captivating. How pretty she was. She certainly had her father's good looks, what characteristics she inherited from her mother she really couldn't work out.

She stood in silent thought, not listening to Joe ramble on, his speech which was taking forever to finish, but thinking of the weekend in Paris with Mike.

How wonderful the time was, how romantic he made it. She felt her neck with her left hand and her carefully manicured finger nails for the beautiful diamond necklace he had given her on the first night there in the hotel room he had so cleverly booked. The view of the city from their hotel window was breathtaking. She thought of the fun and the laughter they had, of the champagne they had drunk and of the passion they had shared.

Then she remembered the bit on the last day, the Sunday just before they were about to leave to catch the plane back, when she told him about her unexpected meeting Polly and 'him'. She remembered how she just stood there, looking at her open mouthed and shocked as if she had told him that his wife was standing behind him.

Of how his shocked face turned to that of red faced anger and then one of disgust.

She remembered soothing him by telling him that 'of course there may be nothing in it, they might just be friends?' and of him replying in a raised voice that 'of course there is something in it. Haven't you heard about him, about his reputation? I've heard the gossip of how he has a countless supply of girls queuing up, he seems to have some sort of contest with himself. After all, you've just told me that you have witnessed others going in and out of his flat - what the hell is he up to?'

She gently bit her bottom lip in thought of how he grabbed his bag in hurried frustration and packed the few things he had bought with him. His obvious desire to return home as soon as possible to confront this child whom she had tried to impress upon him that this 'child' was now a woman, an adult, to behave as she should wish and that nothing he could do - would stop her. That if he issued her demands then he could risk losing her.

But, he was having none of it. He was angry and he wanted to get home to confront her about what she was up to.

Candice knew she stood no chance of appealing to his better nature, to attempt to get him to see how foolish he was being. All she wanted to do was to bring their encounter to his attention, to warn him that his daughter may be involved with a less than accepted beau and that if there was anything in it, to hear it from her rather than some mid morning coffee chat gossip in the control room.

Their flight home was a silent one. Candice was disappointed that her weekend away with the man she so loved had finished this way. She didn't know when she would next have him to herself again. How she wished she had never seen the two of them together.

'You can't tell her I saw them' she had softly said as the flight landed.

'I know' is all he said back.

When he had returned to the house Polly had been out. Old crab had also been out most of the day and so was busy catching up on things she wanted to do before he got home.

'Where's Polly?' he had asked as he walked through the door.

'Oh, charming' his wife had replied. 'Lovely to see you back dear'.

He had looked over in her direction and poured himself a drink, not asking if she would like one.

The old crab tutted and walked huffily off in the direction from where she had come to continue making the bed.

He walked to his office at the rear of the house, which overlooked their beautiful landscaped garden, sat down and tapped his fingernails on the desk to which he was facing, his computer and laptop adorning it. He had then decided perhaps Candice was right. He shouldn't say anything to Polly, not just yet anyway. He was going to gather some facts first. He would turn detective and watch this grease-monkey himself. And when he was sure, he would deal with it. He didn't want to ponder on the thought of this man touching his beautiful, precious and only daughter, he just knew that if he had even dared to, then he would get his revenge. Until then, he would wait. And when he was sure, God help him.

Loud cheering and clapping bought Candice back to reality, to where she was, to the room which was full of friends, colleagues and her lover.

The speech at last being over, the music was started up again and the party continued.

Bernice had decided to confront Mike. She had placed her application form on line and was waiting for acknowledgement of the post she so desired. She was fed up with waiting, knowing that the role should be hers and hers alone. She knew there would be no contest and she also knew that there was a process, a process that had to be followed, just to make sure it was fair.

She saw her chance and without any hesitation went in for the kill.

'Mike, a word please.... about my forthcoming, erm, position'. She knew she had it 'in the bag'. She was more than qualified, more than able and of course being with the Service for so long that held her in good stead.

Her response was not one which she was expecting.

'Ah, Bernice'. He cleared his throat and ushered her into the lobby where it was a little quieter and away from prying eyes.

'Perhaps now is not the right time to discuss any future plans you might wish to make. Indeed, it goes without saying that, although you are highly qualified and able to do the job you say you applied for, there was another contender, one which, shall we say, has shown all the characteristics which we are looking for'.

He knew this wasn't going to be easy. He knew that she would be a hard case to quieten. He had thought long and hard about how he would get round the problem of making sure that Griff got the post and how he could manage to intercept her application and that of any other that might be posted.

He had a friend, one that worked within the IT section. It had cost him dearly but after laying out the money his request to squash any further applications had been carried out. The Board were astonished to be told that only one applicant had applied.

'Well, once I get short listed then I am sure the panel will have no hesitation, no hesitation at all in selecting me' she continued.

'Short listed?   I'm sorry Bernice, I don't think you understand'.

Some late party goers had arrived and were noisily making their way through the lobby to the party. Mike and Bernice separated so they could get through. As the door opened on to the room loud music, laughter and a dropped glass could be heard, only to be quietened again by the door closing after them.

Candice had seen Mike with Bernice as the door had swung open. She didn't know what they were talking about but they seemed in serious conversation and she knew it was best to stay away. Especially as the old crab was around. Mike wouldn't have liked Candice getting too close to him. Not there, not then. How she wished she could be with him tonight but she would have her chance again another time, another place. She was well used to playing second fiddle by now, even though she hated it. Well used to being 'the other woman'.

'Mike?' Bernice was starting to sound on the verge of hysteria.

'Bernice'… Mike once again cleared his throat and so wishing he had another drink in his hand rather than the empty glass he now held very firmly.

'Bernice, the short listing was concluded last week. You weren't on the selection'. A decision was made yesterday and the post has gone to someone else within the Call Centre, the only applicant which applied. Now, if you don't mind, I need to get back to my wife and the party I came here for'. He turned to walk away.

A furious, red faced and shaking Bernice turned also towards his direction.

'I posted my application on the site. It was successful. It was received. I have the email to prove it'.

'No Bernice', he said turning slightly with one hand on the door to re-enter the party room.

'No. Your application was never received. You have obviously made a mistake. The closing date was clearly printed. Your so-called posting was never forwarded and the job has gone to someone else. End of story Bernice. End of'.

'I wont have it, I wont. You'll have to redo the interviews'. She was now on the borders of delusion. Unable to comprehend what had been said by Mike, unable to believe the job she had been waiting so long for had been stolen from her and given to another.

Mike smiled, apologetically. 'Theres nothing anyone can do, not now. The post has been offered and accepted. Which is something you will have to do Bernice, accept it. Accept the fact that you did not apply, did not get short listed, did not have an interview and did not get the position. Accept it and move on'.

'Who DID get it?' She had to know, she had to know who had got the job which was meant to be hers and hers alone. And then come Monday she would be able to voice her protest at H.R. and show the proof that she was an applicant, an applicant that had posted her forms and one which had the proof.

As he walked through the door and with shouts of 'Joe, this way, smile for the camera' he mouthed 'G R I F F'. And then he was gone.

She stood there, paralysed for just a moment. Her back tightly up against the wall, beads of perspiration appearing on her brow and across the palms of her small hands. Her knees felt shaky and she felt sick. She stood there open mouthed facing the direction in which he had left and at that point realised not only was something very strange going on but that the crutch of her knickers were damper than damp, she had in fact virtually wet herself.

Urinating in public was not really the best thing to do, especially when you are at such a private function. She slowly walked towards one of the toilets and locked herself quietly and strangely calmly in a cubicle. Stepping out of the underwear that she had ruined she picked them up and dropped them down the lavatory, flushing them away.

Knickerless and promotionless she stayed there for quite some time, working out her next course of action, trying to make sense of what Mike had just told her.

How come her application was never received? That explained why she hadn't heard from the recruitment processing board. How come Griff, of such little experience, of such a lack in life skills, how come he managed to apply? Move, how did he end up getting it? And why weren't there any other applicants?

Something very strange was going on. And she knew she had to get to the bottom of it. She unlocked the cubicle door and went to the wash basin to wash her hands staring at her reflection back at her in the mirror, a reflection of an older, much older version of her true self, not noticing the other two females along side her chatting away merrily.

She left the facility and headed back to the party, ignoring, not seeing people in her path. She headed for the bar and ordered a very large double whisky and with glass in hand walked back towards the ladies toilets again this time to lock herself away and think. Think of what to do and how to do it.

She glanced at her watch. An hour had elapsed. She needed another drink. She also needed to gain access to a computer.

As she emerged from the ladies toilets she noticed at the far end of the hall there were doors and signs noting 'offices'. She looked around her and found herself alone. She made her move and approached the doors which had signs for 'authorised personnel only'. With one hand on the handle of the first door she found it unlocked and slowly, quietly grasped it letting herself in to the office where she discovered a computer.

Silently making her move to the desk and in dimmed lights, she switched on the machine and sat down in front of it. Access was easy and it allowed her to gain her log on to her emails.

She scrolled down looking for her submitted application. An application she knew she had made and now wishing she had printed off a copy. Further on and on she went, looking searching frantically for her proof until she could search no more. It wasn't there. Mike was right. But she knew she had posted it. She knew she had made the application and more than that she knew it had been successfully received. Why wasn't it there?

She searched again, this time taking longer thinking she may have missed it. But it wasn't there. How could this be? She couldn't have dreamt it. This job meant so much to her and it should have been hers.

She knew she would have to leave the room before being caught in there. She could have been accused of doing anything. As she logged out, puzzled and confused and making sure her tracks couldn't be noticed she realised. She realised very quickly that this was a cover up and that someone had accessed her log in and destroyed her application. That someone would obviously have had to be very clever but more than that, would be very determined.

She knew that person would be Griff.

Having had more to drink than she should have and now engulfed in rage and mis-justice she knew she had to get revenge. The job was gone, gone not just to someone else but to him. A mere boy who was not deserving of it, her junior.

Closing down the computer, so the evidence of her being there disappearing, she slipped out of the room as unnoticed as she had entered and approached the large kitchen on the other side of the all. It was empty although it was obvious there had been staff occupying it, possibly to return at any minute. She walked swiftly, quietly towards the drawers and pulled one open. A large kitchen knife was staring back at her. 'use me, use me, use me' it was saying to her, at that stage, deranged mind.

Engulfed with drunken-ness and anger and armed with a 7" bladed knife up her left sleeve she left the kitchen and returned to the party, to order another very large drink and search out the double-crossing little shit.

She had followed him out to the car park. He had left the party to have a cigarette. Staggering slightly through the alcohol consumption, he found his way to a resting area between to parked cars.

The night was still and the sky clear. As he lit the cigarette he glanced upward and observed the stars twinkling away as if they were winking at him. There was a cool breeze but he found it refreshing after the stuffiness and warmth of the atmosphere from the crowded room from where he had previously been.

He smiled to himself, deep in the knowledge that his newly found promotion would ensure his future success and smug at how he had managed to accomplish it - and so easy too.

He took a long hard drag on the cigarette and flicked the ash out towards one of the cars when he heard the footsteps behind him.

He turned in her direction, surprised at her appearing.

Realising that this could be a confrontation he was ready for her, secure in his confidence now that the alcohol had provided.

Her eyes bore into him. She held no expression.

'Hello Bernice. How nice of you to join me. Care for a cigarette?' His words mocking, sarcastic.

She uttered no reply. She just stood there, staring at him. Anger building away inside her and revenge deep in her thoughts.

'I said, care for a cigarette?' His repeated sentence now a little louder and even more mocking. He held out the opened packet in her direction.

She continued in her refusal to speak, still staring hard into his face, a face she so wanted to punch, hard.

'I take that as a "no" then' he said to her with even more sarcasm. He pulled back the outstretched packed of cigarettes and replaced them in his trouser pocket.

The sound of laughter and faint music could be heard in the distance behind them which the party goers would be dancing along to in the final sages of the retirement function.

'Ha' he said and he turned away from her, leaning on one of the parked cars for support, smiling to himself.

'Silly bitch' he muttered under his breath. Hoping she would go away as quickly as she appeared he dropped what was left of the smoked cigarette onto the ground and used his right foot to extinguish it, grounding it into the tarmac beneath him.

She moved forward slightly, her hand behind her back holding tightly onto the sharp implement she had stolen earlier from the kitchen.

He turned in her direction, ready to return to the party from she they had both come. She appeared to be blocking his way.

'Excuse me' he said to her, attempting to move past.

She didn't move. With a car either side of them he couldn't get past her unless she did move bit it was all to obvious to him now that she didn't intend to.

He briefly considered turning round and walking around the cars to avoid her but her intimidation of not allowing him through was not going to deter him.

'I said excuse me'. His voice now much louder.

Still no movement.

'Look, you stupid bitch, move. I cant get past you unless you do and like hell am I going the other way so either move or I will just push past you'.

Still she continued to just glare at him, her expressionless eyes fixed upon his face as if she were under some form of hypnotic spell. A woman possessed.

'O.K, have it your way'.

And as he moved forward to barge past, she made her move.

The knife appeared quickly, without hesitation. He didn't see it.

All he felt was a surging pain in his side. He stood there, momentarily, staring at her. Questioningly, without voice, frowning slightly. Everything started to appear as if in slow motion.

He felt his body that the knife had penetrated and looked down. She had removed the knife and she stood there with it in her hand, blood dripping from it.

His hand was oozing blood, fresh bright red blood. His blood. The pain was intense. He dropped to his knees and looked up at her.

'What have, what have, what have you done?' He gasped.

Still she continued to stand there, now staring back down at him, a half cocked smile upon her lips. Silently she moved backwards and allowed him to fall onto the ground.

'You got what you deserve' is all she said as he lay there, motionless, blood pouring from his open wound.

Gasping for breath he lay there, unable to shout for help, unable to move.

———

Back at the party, things between Rob and Stephanie were becoming strained. It was obvious to all those around that she had drunk far too much and was talking on a louder level.

Rob was trying to quieten her and attempting to lead her out of the room.

'No, no I wont go, get your hands off me'. Stephanie, defiant and now, because of the alcohol consumption, was becoming more and more confident.

People were starting to look over in the direction of the two people who were obviously arguing, loudly. Whispers were exchanged as to why.

None more so than from Jonny who, even though he was trying so hard to get the mechanic's attention, found that even with his desire to seduce the mechanic once more, he couldn't ignore what might be the cause of this emotional outburst from Stephanie.

The mechanic was standing at the bar, holding a drink in his hand. Bemused at the situation in the corner he cast his attention in that direction too.

Candice moved forward to try and separate the couple, as it was becoming embarrassing to watch.

Stephanie, by this time, was so intoxicated that nothing was going to stop her hatred of mankind.

Candice tried, very hard, to usher her out of the room. Unsuccessfully.

'Whats wrong with you all' she screamed at the audience she had now acquired.

'Cant I have a conservation with my "ex-lover" then?' Her words not coming out of her mouth as she expected them to.

Brows were raised and questioning whispers between the guests were being made.

'Steph!' Rob rose his voice at her. Warningly, alarmed at what she had revealed. It was too late for nothing anyone could have done would have stopped the process.

The music, now turned down in volume, was low enough for everyone present to hear her next loud and imposing broadcast.

'Oh, didn't you all know?' She sneered at them all.

Rob, looked down at the floor, not knowing what to do.

Candice glanced towards Mike as if he might be able to do something. She was sure what Stephanie was about to say, and she was very sure it wasn't going to be good. Mike wasn't looking back at Candice. He was staring hard at the mechanic.

The mechanic was now staring hard in Polly's direction, longingly and lustfully.

The old crab was staring at Candice, wondering why Candice was always looking over in Mike's direction.

Jonny was staring at Stephanie, wondering what the hell she was talking about. His thoughts about his talk with Polly now at the back of his mind.

'So, shall I tell you then?' Stephanie threw back her head in a small laugh.

'Didn't you all know that it was me that Rob had an affair with? It was me that broke Belinda's heart. It was ME ..... ME, ME, ME'.

Hushed voices were now being heard. All around the guests were whispering, astonished in Stephanie's revelation.

But she wasnt going to stop there.

She turned towards the mechanic, still standing at the bar, still mockingly smiling.

Candice had moved forward to try and calm her. But she was unable to stop her next move.

'So', she continued, looking in the mechanic's direction.

'So, who was it then, who was it then, who was in your bed before I turned up the other day, hey? Do I know her, do any of us know her?'

All eyes reverted then onto the mechanic. He continued to stand there, saying nothing and just smiling, as he always did.

'Come on, don't be shy. You had your fun with me, who else were you shagging then?'

Her voice was bordering hysteria.

The shock of Stephanie being involved in this love triangle was not hitting Jonny just quite yet. He knew at this point that Stephanie was just about to do his job of telling Polly to get stuffed for him. He glanced briefly over to Polly, who had secretly been knocking the wine back without her parents knowledge. Polly was just standing there. She felt the tears stinging her eyes due to the betrayal and the public announcement.

Polly stepped forward, unaware that Jonny had also stepped forward.

And in complete unison both Polly and Jonny said the word together.

'ME'.

Gasps were heard all around the room. People were looking from the mechanic to Stephanie, from Stephanie to Polly, from Polly to Jonny.

Polly looked at Jonny, shattered at his involvement. Jonny stared hard at the mechanic, for support. The mechanic put his glass back on the bar and started to clap. Slowly but loudly.

No-one could believe the disclosure from both the young people at the party. Especially the news from Jonny.

Stephanie dropped to her knees, unbelieving that she had been used to such an extent, not just with him sleeping with one person but two. And the revelation that one of these lovers was a man. Two of her colleagues too. It was all too much for her to bear. She just remained, in a kneeling position, arms clasped around her as in a hug and rocked backwards and forwards. Her life now a shambles. All because of him.

Polly stared long and hard at Jonny. 'What?' She spat the word at Jonny. He just looked back at her, raising an eyebrow in answer.

The mechanic had stopped is lone clapping. And was walking towards the exit.

'What?' The response from Mike was as unexpected as the announcements from all three of them.

Candice just froze. She knew Mike mustn't blow his cover. Old crab froze, she knew Mike mustn't allow the secret out that Polly was his daughter.

As Mike moved towards the mechanic, with all intentions and not thinking it out very carefully with the repercussions of any action, a scream was heard from outside.

One of the guests had left the room for air. She was disgusted at the outburst from Stephanie and especially so as this was Joe's retirement party. How could they all behave so badly?.

In her quest for air she had come across Griff lying in a pool of blood.

Her screams alerted all those at the party and the gathering quickly moved to the car park, all thoughts of the previous antics temporarily forgotten.

———

No-one had noticed that Bernice had disappeared. No-one even gave her a second thought.

The call came into the Control Room and they took the news of a stabbing. The patient was unconscious, not breathing.

They were told that Mike was giving resuscitation to the patient and the call operator, oblivious to the patient's identity, remained on the line until the sirens approached.

The air was full of silence apart from the compressions that Mike was giving Griff.

Stephanie was still on her knees, alone in the party room. Music was still being played. She was sobering up, quickly. She realised what her earlier actions would now imply. Her confession of being the underlying cause of why Belinda took her own life would be the reason she could never return to the Call Centre. As she rocked back and forth she felt the pain in her stomach, the cramping.

She felt the blood between her legs and she knew. She knew her unborn baby was to be lost.

The stunned and shocked audience watched on as the ambulance and the police arrived at the same time from different directions in the darkness and the still of the night.

The outburst and the damaging confessions from Stephanie, for now, at the back of everyone's minds.

The old crab standing silently behind her husband watching him work on the now patient .
Candice standing alongside Mike, watching and feeling totally helpless, Jonny holding her hand, squeezing it gently for support and reassurance.

Polly was sobbing to herself, in a corner of the cold car park, feeling used. She knew her parents would be furious, she knew she might never be allowed back to the call centre for her father would make sure of that. She also knew that her father would do everything in his power to finish the mechanic too. She was pleased. She wasn't sure what he would do but she just knew he would 'fix it'. He had, after all, friends in very high places.

The stretcher was being taken from the back of the ambulance towards the patient. The blue flashing lights from all corners or the car park were bright.

Mike was still giving resuscitation as the crew took over. He hands now red from Griff's blood. He had lost so much. His body cold and limp.

The police officers were rounding up people from the party and asking them questions. Questions that for a very long time people would ask, assumptions made, whispered voices and nudges whenever there was a chance.

And life in the Call Centre would never be the same again.

Lightning Source UK Ltd.
Milton Keynes UK
13 October 2009
144894UK00001B/42/P